Darcy's Honor
A Pride and Prejudice Variation

Victoria Kincaid

Darcy's Honor

Elizabeth Bennet is relieved when the difficult Mr. Darcy leaves the area after the Netherfield Ball. But she soon runs afoul of Lord Henry, a Viscount who thinks to force her into marrying him by slandering her name and ruining her reputation. An outcast in Meryton, and even within her own family, Elizabeth has nobody to turn to and nowhere to go.

Darcy successfully resisted Elizabeth's charms during his visit to Hertfordshire, but when he learns of her imminent ruin, he decides he must propose to save her from disaster. However, Elizabeth is reluctant to tarnish Darcy's name by association…and the viscount still wants her…

Can Darcy save his honor while also rescuing the woman he loves?

ISBN: 978-0-9975530-6-2

For my uncle.

Thank you for reading.

Chapter One

"He has been so unlucky as to lose your friendship, and in a manner which he is likely to suffer from all his life." Elizabeth Bennet's words echoed in Darcy's ears even as he stalked away from the dance floor. They had talked of many things following this pronouncement about Wickham, yet these were the words which haunted him. Wickham had not even attended the Netherfield ball, and still his presence bedeviled Darcy.

That someone as clever and vivacious as Miss Elizabeth could be taken in by the blackguard was a tribute to the man's skill with falsehoods. The man might be good with a pistol, but his best weapon was a constant stream of lies.

I should have stayed to ascertain the nature of Wickham's falsehoods so that I might correct her misapprehensions, Darcy berated himself. *I should know the nature of the lies he has imposed upon her.* But he loathed wallowing in the muck created by Wickham's perfidy, and he had already spent too much of his life cleaning up the man's messes. Really, was it too much to ask of destiny that he never lay eyes on the man again? He would prefer to forget Wickham's very existence.

The lady had not seem disposed to hear the truth of the matter. Her eyes had blazed as she accused him of being a false friend to Wickham. Unfortunately, that angry light made her eyes even more alluring.

Why must he be so drawn to Elizabeth Bennet? Why had he been obsessed with inviting her to dance? Darcy must have conversed with every eligible woman in the *ton*—daughters of dukes and earls—and felt no spark of admiration. Yet attraction blazed into a bonfire in the presence of this country miss with no name to speak of and a completely objectionable family. Obviously she had no thought of exciting Darcy's admiration, or she would not have treated him with such naked disdain. *She would forget Wickham in a heartbeat if she knew how frequently she occupied my thoughts.* But her shock when he requested a dance showed how little she expected his attentions.

She would never know, he vowed, quickening his steps in his flight from the dance floor. He knew perfectly well that she was joining a group of guests on the balcony, yet he was practically running in the opposite direction. Darcy reached the punch bowl and accepted a full glass from the footman who was serving. Dancing had made him thirsty, and he drank almost the whole glass in one gulp.

Glass in hand, he regarded the throngs of Bingley's guests. A new set had formed, and couples were moving through the figures at a brisk pace. On the other side of the room, people talked and laughed, gossiped and waved fans.

I should seek out Mrs. Hurst or Miss Bingley for a set.

But his feet continued to carry him away from the dancing. Neither woman was as light on her feet as Miss Elizabeth, and their conversation was equally lacking. When one wanted beef, gruel would not suffice.

Her eyes were so fine; he had never before seen such a deep and magnificent shade of blue. They sparkled with wit and merriment when she spoke. The arch of her brow when she made a pert remark...and that twist of her lips... Darcy was certain he had never seen a face with so much intelligence or a woman with such lively conversation. In company with most women, Darcy found their conversation depressingly predictable, but he could never anticipate the words uttered by Elizabeth— *Miss Bennet*, he silently corrected himself.

He had almost reached the balcony before he realized it was his destination. But he would take care that Elizabeth would not see him. *I will simply take one more glance at her*, he promised himself. *I will not converse with her, but I will look my fill, and then I can ignore her for the remainder of the evening.* Darcy congratulated himself on his restraint as he approached the doorway to the balcony.

The November weather was exceedingly mild, and Netherfield's ballroom had grown quite warm as the guests danced. The French doors had been thrown wide, and guests wandered freely between the ballroom and balcony.

Darcy paused on the threshold as his eyes instantly found Elizabeth. Then he stepped back into the shadows created by some curtains hanging around the doorway; in this way he could observe her unnoticed. She took his breath away. Her dress was a cream-colored silk figured with embroidered flowers and leaves. She had eschewed an elaborate hat, like the orange horror Miss Bingley boasted; instead, small flowers and ribbons adorned Elizabeth's dark curls. The effect was simple but dazzling.

She moved with a grace and ease that suggested she was completely unaware of how beautiful she truly was. Many in the neighborhood described Jane Bennet as a great beauty, but he could not fathom it. The older sister certainly had the kind of simple prettiness that many women of the *ton* aspired to, but it could not compare to Elizabeth's complicated, dark beauty.

Elizabeth was conversing with a small crowd of people that included her sister Jane and Bingley, standing quite close to each other as usual, as well as Mrs. Hurst and a man Darcy had met for the first time that evening: Henry Carson, Viscount Billington. Lord Henry had an estate in Kent but currently was visiting an aunt, the daughter of an earl, who lived at Felham Hall not far from Netherfield.

The viscount was tall but not particularly well favored. His features were gaunt, with a rather prominent nose. Yet he seemed an amiable enough man and had—not surprisingly—been eagerly sought after as a dance partner.

Elizabeth tipped her head back as she laughed at some words of Bingley's. *Has she ever laughed thus at words of mine?* Darcy was fairly certain the answer was no.

But Darcy was not the only one regarding Elizabeth with intense interest; Lord Henry's eyes were fixed on Elizabeth's face, and he stood closer to her than was seemly. He murmured something to her that evinced a brief smile, but she immediately turned her attention back to Mrs. Hurst's conversation.

Lord Henry shifted his weight so that the sleeve of his coat brushed against her bare arm. She shivered noticeably without turning toward the viscount. Darcy's heart raced, and he dug his fingernails into his palms. *I came to observe; I do not want to draw attention.* The lord's sleeve brushed her arm again—clearly no accident. Darcy was aware of a most ungentlemanlike desire to strike the man. Elizabeth shot Lord Henry a sidelong glance, and he smirked at her; but she did not acknowledge his flirtation, let alone return it. Rather, Elizabeth resumed her attention to the conversation, edging a little closer to her sister.

A small part of Darcy rejoiced at her disinterest and harbored dark thoughts about the viscount. He had never experienced jealousy before but suspected that was the troubling sensation he now felt. *At least Elizabeth shows no interest in Lord Henry, but how long can I expect that to continue?* A viscount would be a brilliant match for a woman like Elizabeth—far higher than anything she might aspire to. Darcy desperately wanted to march onto the balcony, grab Elizabeth by the hand, and take her off to an isolated corner of the house—demonstrating to everyone that she was not available for other men's interest.

What if the lord fell in love with her and made her an offer? There was no hope Elizabeth would decline such a magnificent offer and the accompanying opportunity to become a viscountess. Darcy shuddered, easily picturing Elizabeth married to that man, forever beyond his reach.

A cold shiver traveled down his spine. *I cannot allow it. I must propose to Elizabeth myself.* Darcy envisioned her reaction. She would be so surprised and pleased. He could imagine the arch smile and the fire in those fine eyes—sparkling just for him. He would take her to Pemberley; he could not wait to show her the house—his favorite rooms and secret haunts. She would be a spectacular mistress for Pemberley. Georgiana would adore her.

And he would bring her to his bed. Darcy allowed himself a moment to fantasize about their wedding night—how her lips would taste, how her silky tresses would feel in his fingers…

These images led inevitably to the thought of her body swollen with his child and then to the picture of her holding a baby while a small toddler clung to her skirts. It was a sweet picture indeed…

"I daresay you are as thoroughly disgusted by that display as I am." The sharp voice cut into Darcy's reverie like a knife. Jerking his head to the side, he found Miss Bingley standing next to him, staring out at the balcony. The sudden return to reality was quite abrupt and unwelcome.

Miss Bingley watched her brother and Miss Jane Bennet with narrowed eyes. "Really, she is entirely unsuitable. She is a sweet girl, but that family of hers…" Miss Bingley gave a dramatic shudder. "I had hoped that by now Charles would have lost interest. She is not *that* handsome after all." She rolled her eyes. "But now I worry that she has ensnared him thoroughly, and she does not even appear very happy about it."

Indeed, Jane Bennet's features were serene. The smiles she bestowed on Bingley were no different from those she gave to her sister or Mrs. Hurst.

"I would wager," Miss Bingley continued through gritted teeth, "that she cares nothing for him. Her mother has simply instructed her to find a wealthy husband."

Darcy had no difficulty picturing Mrs. Bennet in that role. And if Jane had received such instructions, surely Elizabeth had as well. Although she had not behaved as if she sought a wealthy husband, the thought diminished her in his eyes. Darcy released his hold on the fantasy of a life with Elizabeth. It was just a silly fantasy after all. And it quickly dissolved.

"Do you wish to take action?" Darcy asked Miss Bingley, gesturing toward Bingley.

She smiled triumphantly. "Indeed. We must separate Charles from Hertfordshire immediately."

Of course! That would solve more than Bingley's problem. If Darcy were no longer near Elizabeth Bennet, surely this foolish yearning would dissipate. "Very well," he said. "We must speak with him tomorrow."

Miss Bingley's mouth curved in a slow smile. "I knew I could depend upon your good judgment." She paused for a moment. "It really is quite warm in the ballroom; I think I shall have some punch." Another pause. She obviously hoped Darcy would take the opportunity to join her, but he did not want anyone's company—least of all Miss Bingley's. After a moment, she turned on her heel and walked briskly back into the ballroom.

Now that he knew this likely was the last time he would ever gaze upon Elizabeth, Darcy found it even more difficult to tear his eyes from her. Why did she have to look so beautiful tonight? Although he had banished the marital fantasy, pieces of it intruded upon his thoughts.

The viscount continued to move closer to her, his hand brushing her elbow. Darcy clutched the edge of the doorway, wishing he could rush out to the balcony and stop the man. *I am not jealous. I do not wish it were my hand touching her skin. I am simply disgusted that she would allow such liberties. If she tolerates such attentions, she must be a fortune hunter after all.*

At that moment, however, Elizabeth gave the viscount a sharp look and stepped out of his reach. Darcy silently cheered, his faith in Elizabeth's character restored. She paid the viscount no heed as she conversed with her sister and Bingley; however, the viscount was regarding her intently under his dark brows with a smirk on his face, showing no sign that he was chagrined at Elizabeth's obvious disinterest. Darcy wanted to give the man a lesson in manners, but it was not his place. In fact, he should leave the vicinity entirely.

Without another glance in Lord Henry's direction, Elizabeth took her sister's arm, and they strolled toward the edge of the balcony with Bingley trailing behind. The move appeared completely natural, and yet Darcy had no doubt it was intended to get Elizabeth beyond the range of the viscount's wandering hands. Darcy wanted to applaud Elizabeth's maneuver; then he wanted to enfold her in his arms.

Lord Henry did not follow the Bennet sisters but watched Elizabeth as a cat watches a mouse. Darcy had some idea of Elizabeth's stubbornness; the viscount would not find it easy to change her opinion of him. No doubt he would soon quit the field in search of a woman who was more easily charmed. Yes. The thought filled Darcy with relief.

Resolutely, he turned away from the delicious sight of her figure outlined against the sky. He must shut the door on that fantasy and forget it had ever existed. If Jane Bennet was unsuitable for Bingley, her sister was doubly so for Darcy.

He must forget her fine eyes and anything they promised.

Chapter Two

Elizabeth had not seen Lord Henry in the fortnight since the ball at Netherfield Park. Those weeks had been tumultuous, occupied with Jane's grief over Mr. Bingley's departure and Elizabeth's refusal of Mr. Collins's offer of marriage—followed by his proposal to Charlotte Lucas. When Elizabeth had spared a thought for the viscount, it was with a sense of relief that he apparently had forgotten her.

But when her family arrived for a ball at Lucas Lodge —in honor of Charlotte's engagement—Elizabeth discovered, to her dismay, that she had not been forgotten. When the viscount caught sight of Elizabeth when she first entered the ballroom, he had examined her from head to toe with what he no doubt thought was flattering attention. But his eyes on her might as well have been spiders crawling on her skin. She had attempted to ignore him, but he approached her immediately.

Her mother had emphasized to all of her daughters the importance of being polite to a peer of the realm, so Elizabeth laughed at his jokes and smiled at his compliments—all the while hoping he would develop an interest in another woman. Kitty and Lydia were determined to be more than polite to the viscount. For two weeks they had spoken of little else besides Lord Henry and the militia. The ball at Lucas Lodge apparently demanded their most daring dresses and their boldest glances.

But Lord Henry's stares seemed reserved for Elizabeth. Even Charlotte had remarked on how fortunate Elizabeth was to be singled out for the viscount's favor. Elizabeth had acquiesced to two dances with him, hoping he would then find another dance partner. Instead, he insisted on bringing her punch and entertaining her with *bon mots*. Her increasingly pointed attempts to distance herself from the man had been countered over and over. It was almost as if he knew she did not wish for his company and regarded it as a challenge. But that could not possibly be the case. What man would wish to impose himself where he was not wanted?

When he requested that she join him in visiting the blue drawing room, she had acquiesced as a means of placating him—with the idea that she could politely decline further discourse with a claim: "Oh, sir, I do not wish to monopolize you when other young ladies would enjoy your company!"

Now that she was in the drawing room, she realized what a mistake she had made.

Elizabeth had not expected the drawing room to be empty. The ball at Lucas Lodge was quite a crush, and Lord Henry had assured her that the drawing room was full of old ladies (including his own aunt, Lady Mary) fanning themselves and gossiping. Elizabeth had no reason to disbelieve him, so she agreed to accompany the viscount so he might show her the portrait over the mantel; he swore the woman in the painting showed a striking resemblance to Elizabeth.

Elizabeth had not been particularly interested in the painting, and even less interested in Lord Henry, but at least she could tell her mother that she had been polite to him.

But the room was unoccupied. Elizabeth was immediately uneasy about being alone with the viscount, particularly after he shut the door. They were alone and unchaperoned. It was odd; being with many other men would not have made her uneasy. She would have had no qualms about Mr. Darcy, for instance, who was always a gentleman even if he was proud and difficult.

Why am I thinking of Mr. Darcy? They have been gone for a fortnight, and he does not even like me. The important task at the moment was extricating herself from the drawing room. *I will see the painting and leave.*

"Hmm…I thought the ladies would be here. Where have they stowed themselves?" the viscount wondered. "Well, no matter, here is the work I spoke of." He gestured grandly to the portrait. Elizabeth did not see a striking resemblance. The woman in the painting was blonde, matronly, and at least forty years of age. Elizabeth would have been amused at the comparison had she not been so alarmed by Lord Henry's behavior. Was the painting a pretext?

Elizabeth could almost feel the weight of the viscount's eyes as he stared at her. She sidled toward the door. "I-I should r-return," she stammered. "Jane will be looking for me." She winced internally at this blatant excuse. Jane was so wrapped up in sorrow over Mr. Bingley's departure that she might not notice Elizabeth's absence until the end of the ball.

Lord Henry matched her step for step, prowling after her like a lion stalking its prey. When she tried to move again, she found he had caught her wrist. "Elizabeth," he breathed. "Surely you know by now how I feel about you."

What a peculiar way of phrasing it. Almost as though he was pretending to declare himself without actually declaring himself. "I fear I do not know how you feel about me, sir." Nor did she wish to. She tried to pull her hand from his grasp but to no avail.

He drew back slightly and cleared his throat. "I…uh…feel very strongly about you."

That hardly clarified the matter. Everything about the situation made Elizabeth uneasy. "I should get back to the ballroom. Perhaps we might continue the conversation there."

He squeezed her wrist more firmly. "No!" He cleared his throat again. "That is to say, what I must speak of cannot be said before others."

She struggled to free her hand. "Sir, I really should—"

One second he was a foot away from her; the next his lips were pressing against hers so firmly it was almost difficult to breathe. His tongue quested at the seam of her mouth—perhaps for entry? How unpleasant!

She tried to pull away, but he gripped her shoulder with bruising pressure. She protested vociferously, but with his mouth on hers, all that emerged were muffled grunts.

Then she heard the worst sound in the world: the door opening. The viscount finally released her, although he continued to grip her hand, and they both turned to face the doorway.

His aunt, Lady Mary, and Elizabeth's mother stood in the doorway, their mouths agape. *What are they doing here?*

Elizabeth expected her mother's shrieks to begin at once, but clearly she was too much in shock. *Perhaps I can forestall the impending attack of nerves with some sort of explanation.*

"Mama, Lord Henry wanted to show me the painting that he thinks I resemble…" Elizabeth gestured weakly to the painting over the mantelpiece. Her mother regarded the portrait dubiously.

Lady Mary chuckled. "Apparently that is not *all* he showed you!"

Lord Henry laughed as well, and Elizabeth restrained an impulse to glare at him.

"This is…this—that is to say, I—" Why could she not form a coherent sentence?

Lord Henry scratched the back of his neck sheepishly. "I fear I got carried away."

Elizabeth glared at him. Why was he implying that they had stolen away to indulge in illicit activities? She would rather kiss a rat!

He gave her a contrite look. "I am so sorry, my dear. I had no intention of letting it go this far, but your beauty…" His voice trailed off as if he could not find adequate words to describe her face.

Elizabeth had been plunged into a mirror world where everything was the opposite of what it should be. Nothing made sense. Why was he speaking so? His every word and glance implied that they had secreted themselves in the drawing room for a liaison.

No matter. All she really wanted was to be rid of the viscount. "I just want to return to the ball," she said.

Finally, the lord released her hand, and Elizabeth hurried toward the door, but her mother caught her by the arm, her eyes wide. "Lizzy, you cannot—! Your dress!"

Only then did Elizabeth glance down at her elegant ball gown. Somehow Lord Henry had managed to pull at the bodice until one sleeve had come completely off her shoulder and halfway down her arm—nearly revealing her breast! The other women had been looking at her the whole time. What must they think of her? What a shame that drawing rooms did not have attached caves where one could hide one's humiliation.

Elizabeth hastily pulled up the sleeve, but there was a small tear in the neckline, and some lace trim was dangling. It would be very noticeable among the crowds at the ball. Elizabeth hastily touched her hair and realized several strands had come loose. Her mother was indeed correct; she could hardly return to the ball in such a state. *What can I do?*

As Elizabeth was frozen in this horrible tableau, a voice called from around the corner. "Mama! Mama! Kitty stole my fan!" Elizabeth closed her eyes briefly, knowing the fresh calamity which was about to descend upon them yet helpless to prevent it. Lydia appeared, moving so swiftly through the doorway that she nearly collided with her mother. She took in the sight of Elizabeth's ruined gown with a chagrined-looking Lord Henry behind her. "Oh!" She clapped both hands over her mouth and convulsed with silent giggles.

It was hardly helpful.

Elizabeth tried to sound more composed than she felt. "Perhaps Charlotte's maid can repair the lace for me…"

Lady Mary regarded Elizabeth with a rather pitying look. "That is the least of your concerns, my dear." Then she turned a harder eye on her nephew. "What are you prepared to do to rectify this situation, Henry?"

Only then did Elizabeth realize the enormity of the event. *They think I...they think we— Oh, heavens, no! They believe I have been compromised by this man!*

"No!" she cried. "Nothing happened. He tried to kiss me; that is all."

Elizabeth's mother apparently did not hear as she chimed in, "Indeed, sir, are you prepared to accept responsibility?" Next to her, Lydia continued to giggle.

No...no...no... Elizabeth wanted to speak, but her throat was completely paralyzed.

"Of course, madam," Lord Henry said smoothly, not looking nearly as abashed as a gentleman caught in a compromising situation should have. "Elizabeth" —she cringed at the sound of her Christian name on his lips —"this is not the way I would have preferred to present you with this question, but would you do me the honor of being my wife?"

The room tilted, and for a moment Elizabeth thought she might faint. She looked from his abashed smile to his aunt's knowing smirk to Lydia's secret glee—and then to her mother's face. Mrs. Bennet's expression of horror had been replaced with wide-eyed excitement at the thought of her daughter wedding a viscount.

Best to immediately forestall any expectations. Elizabeth's gaze returned to Lord Henry. "I thank you for the honor, sir. But I must decline."

But the viscount was already moving closer—as if preparing to embrace her. Now he fell back. "N-no?" His voice cracked. "But you must!"

Even as a small child, Elizabeth had disliked being told what to do; however, she managed to restrain the impulse to stamp her foot. "I do believe I have some say in the matter," she said, attempting to keep her tone light.

"Lizzy!" her mother wailed. "Do not be obstinate now! You must accept his offer. You must see that."

"No, I do not." She folded her arms across her chest and straightened her spine.

Lady Mary shook her head sadly. "You have been compromised, my dear. It might not have been your intention, but you did enter an empty room with a man."

Elizabeth bit the inside of her cheek until the impulse to make a pert remark passed. "I was unaware it was unoccupied, madam," she said.

"And I have not been compromised. We merely exchanged"—her voice faltered, and she cursed her own sense of delicacy —"a kiss."

Lord Henry ran a hand through his hair in frustration, shaking his head. "Elizabeth, my aunt will not believe that. She knows how long we were in here alone. 'Twas at least half an hour."

Lady Mary frowned. "Half that time would be sufficient to ruin a lady's reputation."

What? "Why do you say that, sir?" Elizabeth had journeyed even further into that mirror world. Up was down, and left was right. "We have been here a mere five minutes."

He grimaced. "It was half an hour. We might as well admit the truth."

Surely it had not been…had she lost all sense of time? "No. It was not so long—" Elizabeth gazed imploringly at her mother. "Mama, you know it was not so long."

She shrugged. "I did not mark your departure, Lizzy. I cannot say." Elizabeth wondered if her mother spoke the truth, or if she was taking an opportunity to shackle her daughter to a viscount.

"Lydia…?" Elizabeth looked at her sister desperately.

"La! I have been much too busy dancing to notice you!" Lydia waved her hand about airily.

"No…it was not so long…" But shock had robbed her words of any power. Her denial sounded more like a whine.

The viscount tried to take her hands again, but she clasped them behind her back. "I apologize, Elizabeth. I had no intention of being so ungentlemanly—or of taking something from you that could not be replaced."

Lydia giggled at Lord Henry's words. Elizabeth shook her head again and again. "No…you took nothing…"

The viscount continued to give her a fond, pitying look. Why was he implying they had—? It did not make sense.

"Lizzy," her mother said sharply and pulled Elizabeth to one side of the room, near the fireplace. Lydia followed behind. Mrs. Bennet spoke in an urgent whisper. "Lizzy, you must understand! If word spreads about this encounter, you will be unmarriageable."

Elizabeth regarded Lydia's smirking face; there was no doubt the story would be spread far and wide. "You might as well take this opportunity," her mother continued. "After all, he is a viscount!"

How could she explain her dislike of the man? He always appeared thoroughly charming and completely unobjectionable. In fact, he was unfailingly polite and far more pleasant than Mr. Darcy. And yet, somehow, Elizabeth almost wished Mr. Darcy were here instead. Although the man was unbearably rude, he was honest—sometimes to a fault. He would tell the truth about how long they had been alone together.

Of course, he never would have been caught trying to kiss her. The idea was laughable. *Why am I thinking about Mr. Darcy at a time like this?*

The most important task at the moment was making her mother understand. "Mama, I do not want to marry Lord Henry. I do not like him."

"Poo!" Her mother waved the objection away. "He is quite charming. Everyone enjoys his company. As your acquaintance deepens, you will come to like him more and more. And just think of his income! Such things you can purchase—the jewels, the carriages!"

Elizabeth had no particular objection to jewels and carriages, but the price was far too dear. "I cannot marry him," she said in her firmest voice.

"Lizzy, you must consider your family. The shame would be—"

"Have you ladies reached a conclusion?" Elizabeth looked up, startled. Lord Henry loomed over them, and she had not even heard him approach.

Mrs. Bennet pasted on an ingratiating smile. "Of course, Lizzy will accept your most generous offer."

"No, I will not," Elizabeth said firmly to her mother.

Mrs. Bennet's smile lost a little of its luster as she addressed the viscount. "Perhaps Lizzy *will* need some additional time to decide, your lordship. This is all quite sudden."

Lady Mary snorted, a sound that did not reinforce Elizabeth's opinion of the woman's ladylike qualities. "What is there to decide?" the viscount's aunt asked. "The chit has been compromised. She has no choice!"

Elizabeth felt her insides shrink at this pronouncement. No, it cannot be true. That one unwanted kiss could not have stolen away her future. She still had a choice, did she not?

Lord Henry made a conciliatory gesture in his aunt's direction. "Now, Aunt Mary, I would hazard a guess that Elizabeth feels uncomfortable—with the situation and with me." Elizabeth sighed in relief. *He understands!* "And it was so terribly mortifying to be found in such a compromising position." *Very well, perhaps he did not understand after all.*

Elizabeth cleared her throat. "I truly do not believe I need additional time to—"

It was as if she had not uttered a word. The viscount smiled benevolently at her. "Take all the time you need, Elizabeth," he said grandly, as if all human history were his to grant. "I do not blame you for having doubts." He leaned forward, leering at her. "But I will not promise to not attempt to change your mind."

Elizabeth shuddered.

"And, of course," he continued, "I can do nothing about idle gossip."

Elizabeth's eyes slid to Lydia. There was no hope that her youngest sister would keep this silent. Furthermore, her mother and Lady Mary were two of the greatest gossips Meryton had ever seen. Despair wrapped around Elizabeth's heart and squeezed. The consequences of this evening would be plentiful and far-reaching.

Why did Lord Henry imply they had spent more time together alone than they had? Did he not understand the effect it would have on her reputation? She felt an abrupt swooping sensation as if she sat in a boat in strong swells. Elizabeth had to grasp a chair for balance.

My reputation is ruined.

I am ruined.

The realization crashed over her like a great wave, leaving her alone and desolate in its wake. Her future unfolded before her in horrifying images. Decent men would shun her company. Malicious gossip about her would circulate throughout Meryton. Women would whisper and laugh behind their hands as she passed. Men would smirk. Invitations would dry up. And, worst of all, her family would share in her fate.

Elizabeth bit her lip hard, trying to keep tears at bay.

All that could be avoided if she accepted Lord Henry's offer.

She looked at the viscount again. He was smiling. No doubt it was intended to be sincere and reassuring, but there was a gleam in his eye that belied any attempt at sincerity.

She knew in that instant: he was enjoying himself.

He enjoys trapping me and giving me no choice. He revels in this. It turned her stomach, and for a moment she was in danger of casting up her accounts.

That was why he had made no attempt to exonerate her or salvage her reputation. He relished how it granted him power over her. Perhaps he had even arranged the evening so they would be caught. But why? Was it possible he sincerely loved her? Elizabeth was dubious, but she supposed it was possible. However, she knew she could not trust a man who could maneuver her so easily and manipulate her for his own ends. And where there was no trust, there could never be love.

Well, there was no point delaying the inevitable. She must give Lord Henry her absolute refusal.

Her mother must have guessed the impending response, for she took Elizabeth's hand and dragged her toward the door, ushering Lydia out before them. "In such matters, Lizzy can be terribly indecisive!" she cried to the viscount. "And this honor is so unexpected! I pray you, give her some time to think on it."

The viscount smirked. "Of course! I can wait to claim my prize." His eyes practically caressed Elizabeth. "I can be patient because I know she will be mine eventually."

Her mother smiled as if this declaration of possession were the most romantic thing she had ever heard.

The greedy expression on Lord Henry's face was the last thing Elizabeth saw before closing the drawing room door behind her.

Chapter Three

Life would be easier, Darcy reflected, if everything did not prompt recollections of Elizabeth Bennet. It had been two months and six days since he had last set eyes on her, and yet she continued to haunt his thoughts.

The sight of Bingley recalled Elizabeth's family at the Netherfield ball. Miss Bingley's presence recalled Elizabeth because of her jealous asides and snide remarks. Georgiana reminded him of Elizabeth because he constantly mused how the two women would enjoy each other's company. Even Darcy House itself provoked him into thoughts about Elizabeth. What would she think of the prints in the hallway or the lemon biscuits the cook made for tea?

Darcy had long ago admitted to himself that he was a pathetic mess. Despite having no information about Elizabeth for more than two months, her presence pervaded his life. Naturally, his fascination with the woman would fade with time, but it was lingering far longer than he had anticipated.

Desperation had driven him to join Georgiana in the yellow drawing room as she entertained Bingley and his sisters. Usually he avoided Miss Bingley and Mrs. Hurst whenever possible, preferring to see Bingley at their club, but today he had hoped his annoyance with Miss Bingley would help to make him forget his memories of pert smiles and glossy black curls.

The plan had worked admirably at first. He had been driven to distraction by the woman's incessant prattling about the new style of lace flounces and gossip about people he barely knew.

There was another form of distraction: Georgiana had also invited her friend, Lenora James. Darcy guessed his sister hoped that he would make a match with Lenora. This was the third time he had encountered Miss James, and he was again struck by her beauty. She was also charming, intelligent, and a good conversationalist. Her family was good *ton* and well liked. In fact, if Darcy were to write a list of characteristics he sought in a wife, Miss James would fulfill each criterion admirably.

He had tried to like her. He had.

He had listened attentively to her conversation, which was well-informed and clever; she did not simply pass along gossip or describe her search for the perfect gloves. He had laughed at her jokes and complimented her beauty, all the while musing about how she was his perfect match in every way.

Yet he did not care for her.

Someday they might be good friends, but now he could only catalog the ways in which she was not Elizabeth. She smiled at him. It was quite a pretty smile, and he returned it with a grin that showed as much sincerity as he could muster. But he felt nothing special when he gazed upon her.

He could not help comparing her to Elizabeth. Miss James was a far better candidate for marriage in every respect. Why could he not feel some spark of attraction to her? What kind of spell had Elizabeth Bennet cast over him?

Such thoughts had been whirling around inside his head for months, filling him with unease. He was irritable with the staff and short with Georgiana. She had asked him more than once what was amiss, and he had demurred. He was full of a restless energy that pushed him to take long walks outside, even in cold weather. Yet his appetite had diminished, and he had lost weight. It was intolerable, but Darcy did not have the least idea how to ameliorate the situation.

Not wishing to give rise to false hopes, Darcy turned his attention away from Miss James. Miss Bingley was still speaking with a rhythm that was almost hypnotic. Darcy's attention began to wander as his head dipped lower and lower until it nearly rested on his chest.

"…Meryton…" Darcy was pulled out of somnolence with an abrupt jerk. Was Miss Bingley discussing Hertfordshire? "….A letter from Anna Hopkins," Miss Bingley said to her sister. "You remember her?"

Mrs. Hurst tittered. "Does she still maintain a correspondence with you? Apparently she remains under the delusion that she will obtain an invitation to Bingley House."

Miss Bingley flicked open her fan with a snap, only to employ the object rather lazily. "Heaven knows. I certainly do nothing to encourage the acquaintance," she sneered. "However, the missive did include one item of note." Her glance flickered toward Darcy as if to ensure he was paying proper attention. "About the Bennets. You remember them, Louisa?"

Such a disingenuous act! Darcy ground his teeth together. No one from the Netherfield party was likely to forget the family that Bingley had nearly married himself into. Even Georgiana watched with wide eyes, having heard stories about the Bennets of Hertfordshire.

"What about them?" Bingley asked, hastily setting down his teacup.

His sister took a languid sip of tea, making a great show of indifference. "Charles, you will be very pleased we are gone from that neighborhood and have no more acquaintance with that family. It is an absolute disgrace!"

A chill raced down Darcy's spine. What had happened to the Bennets?

"What is?" Bingley asked impatiently.

"Miss Elizabeth Bennet." Miss Bingley avoided glancing at Darcy as she spoke, yet he had no doubt her words were intended to wound him. He clenched his fists to forestall any impulse to cry out at her.

Instead, he waited while Bingley demanded, "What about Miss Elizabeth?"

His sister shook her head sadly. "Such a disgrace. I do not know how the family will ever recover."

Darcy could hold out no longer. "What has happened?" he finally growled.

The triumphant smile on Miss Bingley's face hardly registered. "Eliza Bennet was caught with that oily viscount—"

"Henry Carson, Viscount Billington," Darcy supplied automatically.

"Yes, that was the name. They were found in a"—she coughed delicately —"compromising position during a ball at Lucas Lodge."

A tight hand seemed to squeeze Darcy's heart.

"Oh dear!" Miss James's exclamation was half distressed and half amused.

Mrs. Hurst tsked. "I confess I cannot be surprised. The whole family had no sense of decorum. The way her younger sisters carried on with the officers! And her mother's behavior. Quite shocking."

"Indeed." Miss Bingley nodded her agreement. "I would not be surprised if her mother arranged the situation to entrap the viscount."

The fist around Darcy's heart closed even more tightly and painfully.

"Naturally," Miss Bingley continued, "Lord Henry did the proper thing and made her an offer."

No, Darcy wanted to cry out, but he had no breath. Mrs. Bennet might be capable of such a maneuver, but Elizabeth would never consent to be part of such a plot.

Mrs. Hurst pursed her lips disapprovingly. "So they are now betrothed?"

Good Lord, no!

Had his heart stopped beating altogether? He must have uttered some sound; Miss James regarded him oddly.

Miss Bingley straightened her shoulders, appearing to be at a loss for the first time. "That would be the sensible course, but…no. Anna Hopkins said the viscount proposed, but Elizabeth declined." Mrs. Hurst's mouth dropped open. "But I cannot be convinced of the accuracy of this account. Why would she decline such a man?"

A swell of relief flooded Darcy's veins. Elizabeth was not married, or even betrothed. *She is not lost to me.* But relief was tempered by anxiety over what she had experienced. Had the man hurt her? What had she suffered?

Mrs. Hurst tossed her head. "If the man's reputation is at stake, perhaps she hopes delay will increase the marriage settlement."

Miss Bingley nodded sagely. "That is precisely the kind of strategy I would expect from such a woman." Darcy had not known it was possible, but he now disliked Miss Bingley even more.

"She did not strike me as a calculating woman." Bingley shifted in his chair.

Miss Bingley waved dismissively. "You are always looking for the best in people, Charles." Her tone suggested that this was a serious character flaw.

"How fortunate we are no longer in that neighborhood." Mrs. Hurst folded her hands in her lap. "Such shocking behavior would have forced us to give up the acquaintance, and it would have been so awkward."

"Indeed. I always loathe being put in the position to cut people. It is so wearing on my nerves," Miss Bingley agreed.

"Quite distressing." Mrs. Hurst nodded.

"I get quite faint thinking about it," Miss Bingley said. "We had a fortunate escape."

Recalling the interactions between Elizabeth and the viscount at the Netherfield ball, Darcy was quite certain she had not sought the man's attentions. If anyone had been entrapped, it was not Lord Henry. Unfortunately, gossipmongers always blamed the woman. Darcy's heart was heavy as he imagined Elizabeth's fate. The weight of disapproval would be crushing—no matter where she ventured.

"We do not know the circumstances," Darcy found himself saying. "Perhaps Miss Elizabeth was not at fault."

Bingley nodded vigorously, but his sister merely regarded Darcy with raised eyebrows. "It is the woman's duty to help keep the man's baser nature in check." She fanned vigorously. "Of course, only if she is so inclined." Darcy bristled at the implication, but Miss Bingley continued. "No doubt we will get word soon that she has contracted a marriage with Lord Henry."

"Perhaps she does not wish to marry him," Darcy ventured.

Miss James covered her mouth in shock as if such a thought was unimaginable. It did not endear her to Darcy.

Mrs. Hurst and Miss Bingley exchanged a glance as though agreeing that he was insufferably idealistic. Mrs. Hurst appeared to stifle a giggle.

"She will have no choice," Miss Bingley said. "No one else would have her. She must accept the viscount or suffer eternal scandal."

"How terrible!" Georgiana's hand covered her mouth. *Of course!* Darcy chastised himself for being blind. Elizabeth's situation naturally reminded his sister of the near disaster at Ramsgate.

Miss Bingley barely managed not to roll her eyes at Georgiana. "Hardly. She will be elevated to a social position far above what she deserves."

Darcy wondered what kind of position Miss Bingley imagined Elizabeth "deserved."

"*He* could do better, of course," Mrs. Hurst said.

Miss Bingley gave her a sidelong glance. "Yes. His estate is rather small, but still, he *is* a viscount. It is unfortunate that he so closely resembles a greyhound."

The sisters both tittered behind their fans at these daring words, and Miss James joined in. At that moment Darcy decided she was not quite as pretty as he had once believed. Georgiana was stone-faced.

Elizabeth being imposed upon by such a man…facing the ruin of her reputation. It was too horrible to imagine. How long would she hold out before agreeing to marry the blackguard?

Elizabeth. His heart ached. He wanted to jump on his horse, ride to Meryton, and…what? He pictured embracing her and holding her safe within his arms, but his imagination went no further than that.

Mrs. Hurst rolled her eyes. "Alone with a man! What did she expect?"

Darcy was suddenly on his feet. "Miss Elizabeth deserves our sympathy, not our condemnation."

Everyone in the room regarded him with open mouths and wide eyes, although Georgiana had a faint smile upon her lips.

Bingley cleared his throat. "Indeed. We must not rush to judgment when we remain unaware of the particulars."

Miss Bingley sneered at her brother but said nothing.

Darcy could no longer sit in the drawing room, calmly sipping tea and discussing Elizabeth's fate as if it were of no importance. The walls were too close; it was too warm, too full of people. He glanced from face to face, wishing he could devise an acceptable excuse, but his brain was not functioning as it should. "Forgive me," he said, not looking at anyone in particular. "I suddenly recalled some correspondence that must be written today."

With that falsehood on his lips, Darcy strode from the room.

***

Rather than going anywhere near his study, Darcy headed straight for the front door. Pausing only long enough to retrieve his greatcoat and hat from the footman, he hurried out of the house and down the steps, quickly falling into the rhythm of a fast walk that carried him away from Darcy House. He kept his head down, eyes fixed on the uneven slate of the pathway, and pulled his hat brim lower on his head. He had no desire to be recognized by a casual acquaintance and forced to endure a conversation about the weather.

The wind stung the exposed skin of his face, and tension in his neck warned of a nascent headache, but he should suffer that—and far more— for what he had done, or failed to do. *If only I had succumbed to the urge to make her an offer that night at Netherfield! Then she would have been safe from the viscount and his schemes. Then she would be mine.*

Instead, she faced marriage to Lord Henry or ruination. It was inevitable that she would accept the viscount's offer. Her reputation had been compromised so thoroughly that the story was bandied about even in London. No doubt the viscount pretended his proposal was an exceptionally magnanimous gesture. She would accept it and be expected to show gratitude.

Darcy's stomach churned, and for a moment he feared he would cast up his accounts in a nearby bush. *My Elizabeth forced into such a position! Her pert smile and fine eyes the property of a man who had entrapped her.*

For Darcy had no doubt about what had occurred despite Miss Bingley's interpretation of the events. He could not forget the night of the Netherfield ball; Elizabeth had not shown the least interest in the viscount's "charms." The lord, on the other hand, had been obsessed with her, regarding her disinterest as a challenge.

Darcy shuddered. He knew men like that, although they usually preyed on women of a lower station. And, of course, their object was not an honorable marriage. *I should have intervened at the first sign of the viscount's unwanted intentions; she deserved my protection. But I was too intent on convincing myself that I cared nothing for her. What a futile endeavor. And now she is ruined and forever beyond my reach!*

If someone had reached into his chest and pulled out his heart, they could not have created a hollower sensation. Months ago he had suspected he might love Elizabeth Bennet, but only now did he realize how deeply the feelings ran. Only now did he recognize the paltriness of his objections to her. Her family, her station, her lack of lineage meant nothing when faced with the prospect of losing her forever. If only he could rewind the hands of the clock! He would give his entire fortune to return to that moment when he walked away from her at the Netherfield ball.

His feet had brought him to Hyde Park. There was no snow on the ground, but the Serpentine was frozen solid. He rambled along the path that paralleled the pond's curves. Fortunately, the chilly air kept most other walkers at home, and he enjoyed a solitary ramble.

Providence provided me with the perfect opportunity: the woman I have been seeking all my life. But only when it is forever lost to me do I appreciate the gift. He savagely kicked a stone from the pathway, and it skittered into a bush.

I am a fool.

Only when a nearby pigeon fluttered away in a panic did Darcy realize he had uttered the words aloud.

He hunched over, digging his hands deeper into his pockets, seeking warmth. *I held a diamond in my hand but treated it like a common rock. I had the opportunity to protect her and secure my happiness, and I let it slip away upon the slimmest of grounds.*

Darcy sank onto a stone bench, the surrounding cold seeping into his bones through his coat. Were his cousin Fitzwilliam present, he would laugh and remind Darcy that there were other women in the world, but that thought only made him queasier. The thought of paying court to another woman…finding another woman attractive without comparing her to Elizabeth… It was unfathomable, an impossible hope. And yet he must find a woman to marry and provide an heir for Pemberley. Picturing another woman in his bed, he experienced more than a little nausea. He imagined thirty years of living with this other woman, and the nausea grew. A lifetime of looking into some other woman's eyes. How could he endure it?

If Elizabeth accepted the viscount's offer, it would be a terrible mistake, but how could he convince her of it when he would never see her again? It would be highly improper to write her a letter. Further, could he, in good conscience, recommend her to refuse the viscount? And, of course, refusal would condemn her to a lifetime of solitude and shame.

In addition, Darcy had no standing in her life to convince her to reject the man. He was not a relative or even much of a friend. Darcy snorted a laugh. Indeed, the only honorable way to convince her to refuse the other man would be to propose to her himself.

Darcy stilled. He stared at the ice of the Serpentine as a cold breeze swirled around his legs.

I could make her an offer.

His mind turned over the possibilities.

There would be a scandal, of course. But Elizabeth would suffer far fewer cuts as Mrs. Darcy than as plain Elizabeth Bennet. The very act of making her an offer would be perceived as Darcy's endorsement of her innocence and virtue. No few of Darcy's relations would be appalled, but he was master of Pemberley and not beholden to their opinions. If members of the *ton* expunged him from their invitation lists, Darcy would not regret the loss.

Darcy would undoubtedly suffer some loss of reputation; the thought pricked his pride. His aunt and uncle would be scandalized that the Darcy name was dragged through the mud. Yet he must weigh that scandal against a lifetime of regret. The distaste at the thought of being ostracized from the *ton* easily gave way when compared to the heavy despair prompted by thoughts of losing Elizabeth from his life forever.

Darcy conjured his father's face in his imagination. *What would Papa advise?* Long ago, in a conversation by the drawing room fireplace at Pemberley, his father had drawn a useful distinction between reputation and honor. *My reputation might be tarnished, but my honor will remain intact as long as I know I have done the right thing.*

As he gazed up at the sky, a pale winter sun finally broke through the heavy gray clouds. An omen? Yes, he could do this. He could be the one to free Elizabeth from the depths of her despair. Darcy pictured her face, alight with surprise and delight when he made his offer. He savored the image.

Undoubtedly she had noticed his interest, but she could not have hoped for an offer even under the previous circumstances. And now she had sunk even lower. She would not expect anything from him. He could imagine her rapture—her gratitude—when he offered to lift her from her misery. The light in those fine eyes would shine just for him.

But he must make his offer soon—before she was compelled to accept the viscount.

Darcy shot to his feet and strode back to Darcy House. He could not delay for even an hour.

Chapter Four

Despite the best efforts of Meryton's vicar, Mr. Lehigh, Elizabeth refused to regret attending church. Sunday services were the only refuge remaining to her outside of Longbourn itself. After the incident at Lucas Lodge, word of her "disgrace" spread quickly. Many doors were closed to her. Invitations to dinners and parties had been revoked, and the young women of the neighborhood were "not at home" when Elizabeth paid a call. After only a few such incidents, Elizabeth found it too mortifying to even attempt to keep up such acquaintances.

Accompanying Elizabeth on walks into Meryton, Kitty, Lydia, and Mary would be subject to stares and whispers. Finally, their mother had forbidden Elizabeth from taking any trips into town. Her only activity now came in the form of long solitary rambles through the countryside.

Elizabeth had considered church to be the one place she could venture with impunity. Even supposedly fallen women were permitted to repent and enjoy God's forgiveness, were they not? Naturally, she had anticipated raised eyebrows and shocked murmurs. She had not expected to hear sermons on the evils of the flesh…three Sundays in a row.

She had gritted her teeth through the first sermon and nearly laughed at the ridiculousness of a second sermon on the same subject. But after the third, she felt more and more as if everyone in the church were staring at her. Elizabeth had been determined to attend church despite her discomfort, but now she wondered if Mr. Lehigh would continue such sermons until she stopped Sunday services altogether. Surely there were parishioners who had committed other kinds of sins and were in need of chastisement! Was there not some soul who had failed to honor his father and mother? Or who had coveted his neighbor's ox?

Elizabeth sighed. Customarily her courage rose with each attempt to intimidate her, but she was not sure she was equal to the hostility of the entire parish—and the vicar—every week.

The stares and condemnation likely would cease if she accepted Lord Henry's offer of marriage. The irony threatened to choke her. She was not actually a fallen woman now, but Meryton would consider her innocence redeemed if she surrendered her virtue to the viscount.

Despite the urge to slide down in the pew, Elizabeth held her head high and affected an air of earnest piety. In reality she was counting the minutes until the service's conclusion. Not for the first time Elizabeth considered whether she should leave Hertfordshire for an extended trip.

Immediately after the incident, Elizabeth set out in earnestness to clear her name, proclaiming her virtue to anyone who would listen. She quickly realized her guilt or innocence was of no real importance. Nobody really knew if Lord Henry had compromised her virtue; the *appearance* of her lost purity was all that mattered. The good people of Meryton felt obligated to act as if she were a fallen woman, whether they believed it to be the case or not.

Elizabeth had always prided herself on an ability to see the good in any situation, but her current position sorely tried her optimism. She was not even certain how many members of her own family believed her assertions of innocence. When she explained what had truly happened, Kitty and Lydia merely giggled while Mary pontificated about the importance of a woman's virtue. Her mother had waved away any explanations and continued to insist that she accept the viscount's offer. Only her father and Jane believed every word of her tale. However, her father did not take the situation seriously and insisted that the gossip would fade eventually, something Elizabeth thought increasingly unlikely.

Jane had been steadfast in her support throughout the terrible trial. When her father had declined to attend church, Elizabeth's mother and sisters declared they had no interest in sitting near the object of such disapprobation, but Jane had not wavered from Elizabeth's side. Although she worried about hurting Jane's reputation, Elizabeth was very grateful. Withstanding the shame without Jane's support would have been far more difficult. As if sensing her discomfort, Jane leaned over in the pew and patted her hand.

Suddenly, everyone around her climbed to their feet and started singing. Elizabeth had lost track of time. It was the recessional hymn; the service was over. *Thank Heavens!*

Elizabeth clambered to her feet with a hymnal in hand but did not sing. She considered the possibility of leaving Meryton. Although she hated to be chased from her home by such a man as the viscount, her family would be less ostracized in her absence. If Elizabeth visited the Gardiners in London for a few months, perhaps the outrage would diminish. She fiddled with a ruffle on her dress, deep in thought. She needed to consider her family. What would happen if her family became completely isolated from good society? What if her presence made it impossible for her sisters to make good matches? Gritting her teeth, she blinked away tears; she was finished crying over the situation.

Jane put away her hymnal and took a step toward the aisle, but Elizabeth gestured to hers as though she wished to stay and read through the hymns. Her sister nodded, understanding that Elizabeth had no desire to join the crowds shuffling out of the church. Jane gave her hand a brief squeeze and then slipped out of the pew. Elizabeth kept her eyes fixed on the hymnal as if it offered the secret to eternal life.

Finally, the church was mostly empty. Elizabeth stood and hurried down the aisle toward the door. If luck was on her side, Mr. Lehigh would be speaking with someone, and she could slip past him, avoiding his accusatory looks. She blinked as her eyes adjusted to the bright sunshine outside. Parishioners clustered in the churchyard, talking and laughing. Elizabeth viewed the crowd, calculating how best to skirt the gathering to reach the road.

Fortunately, Mr. Lehigh was absorbed in conversation with a tall, dark-haired man. Elizabeth ducked her head as she prepared to walk around the pair but nearly stumbled when she recognized the other man.

It was Mr. Darcy.

Elizabeth managed to stifle a groan. As if she did not already have enough trouble!

***

Darcy had always thought of church as a place of refuge from worldly cares. He was not accustomed to feeling angry during Sunday services, but from the moment he settled into a pew near the back of Meryton's small, stone-clad sanctuary, Darcy's ire had been growing. Seated near the front, Elizabeth had not noticed his entrance, but he had witnessed how the good men and women of the congregation stared at her. No one stopped to speak with her or her sister Jane; in fact, they avoided the sisters' pew as if they carried the plague.

Even Mrs. Bennet and the other sisters were seated on the other side of the church. How could they abandon their own family at such a time? Darcy knew he would avoid speaking with Mrs. Bennet after the service; he could not trust himself to keep a civil tongue.

These observations had set his temper at a low simmering boil, and then Mr. Lehigh started his sermon. There was no doubt about the target of his lecture about "fallen women." The sermon's intended audience could not have escaped the notice of anyone save the very youngest children fidgeting in their mothers' laps. Yet Elizabeth had held her head high throughout the entire wretched screed. Darcy could not imagine what it cost her.

Once the service was over, Darcy practically leapt out of his pew in his eagerness to converse with the vicar. With prodigious self-control, Darcy refrained from yelling at the man, but he did suggest several more appropriate topics for future sermons, such as "he who is without sin should cast the first stone" and "Jesus's love for the sinner." Recognizing Darcy immediately, Mr. Lehigh had borne the chastisement with tight lips but no complaints. Indeed, when Darcy finished speaking, the shameless man had several suggestions for how Darcy could use his fortune to benefit the church.

From the corner of his eye, Darcy saw Elizabeth scurrying down the aisle. If only Mr. Lehigh would stop speaking so Darcy could intercept her! But the man prattled on, and Elizabeth sailed right past them with her head bowed and eyes fixed on the ground. He quashed a sense of disappointment. She might not have noticed him, or she sought to avoid an unpleasant encounter with the vicar.

When Darcy managed to wrest himself free from the man's conversational clutches a few minutes later, he scoured the church grounds.

But Elizabeth was nowhere to be found.

***

When Elizabeth was safely past Mr. Darcy, she sighed in relief. Surely he knew of her disgrace by now. No doubt he would have something cutting to say on the subject of fallen women. No, such nasty asides were more Miss Bingley's style. Mr. Darcy would treat her with a brittle courtesy that left Elizabeth with no doubt what he truly thought of her character. She quickened her steps; there was no need for an added dose of humiliation.

Once outside the church, Elizabeth knew better than to approach any of the small knots of parishioners. Her reception would range from coldness to thinly veiled disdain to outright hostility. When such treatment had started, she bitterly resented the unfairness; now she was accustomed to it, even if it exhausted her.

Her mother and sisters were nowhere in evidence. They must have started the walk homeward, either to avoid a cold reception from their neighbors or Elizabeth's company. Elizabeth had hoped Jane would remain, but their mother may have prevailed on her to depart. It was just as well.

She looked over the brown grass near the church and the gray, fallow fields beyond, dotted with vestiges of old snow. She could bear the deprivation. It was for the best that nobody would be seen with her. The walk back to Longbourn was no further than the walk *to* church had been.

It just felt that way.

***

As Darcy rode for Netherfield, he was grateful that Bingley had offered the use of the house; he was in no mood to rub shoulders with strangers at an inn. But there was no reason for him to experience Elizabeth's disregard as a snub. She had no hopes of him and would be embarrassed by the scandal. He must approach her in such a way that left her in no doubt about his benevolent intentions.

"Miss Elizabeth, now that scandal has been attached to your name…"

No.

"I heard that you have been disgraced and…"

No.

"It is my understanding you might be in need of such rescuing as I can provide…"

No.

"Miss Elizabeth, I throw myself at your feet in a desperation of love."

Definitely not, although that sentiment might be closest to the truth.

The scheme had sounded so reasonable in his head during the ride from London, but now he could think of no polite and gracious way to address the scandal. Of course, he could visit Longbourn, but that would hardly be the place to reveal what he knew of her situation. Darcy kicked his horse into a trot. He would need to consider the best approach.

Damnation.

Chapter Five

Since it was not pleasant to observe their neighbors ignoring her, Elizabeth had developed the habit of staring at the road as she walked. Which was why she did not notice Lord Henry until he was almost on top of her.

He had come to call twice at Longbourn since that horrible day at Lucas Lodge. Both times he had pressed her for an answer to his proposal. Both times Elizabeth had told him she was not inclined to accept, but he had behaved as though she were still deciding, which naturally pleased her mother. The viscount had been charming and gentlemanly in Longbourn's drawing room, but Elizabeth had not been sanguine that he would behave honorably if they were alone.

Upon seeing him, she started violently but then increased her pace. Perhaps he would ignore her if she ignored him. However, the viscount immediately reined in his horse so that he blocked the road before her. She stopped, regarding him with narrowed eyes.

"Miss Elizabeth." He nodded.

"Lord Henry." She nodded in return but did not curtsey; the man deserved no such honor.

Shoving her hands deeper into the pockets of her pelisse, she willed them to stop trembling. If only she could maneuver around his horse and continue on her way! But she had no desire to have the viscount at her back. With the man on horseback, at least he could not easily touch her.

"I have been to Longbourn, but you were not at home."

The simple statement chilled her to the bone. She hated the thought that the viscount was looking for her; she had been praying he would forget her existence.

"I was at church," she said, immediately berating herself for being obvious.

"I have not laid eyes upon you for well over five days." He gave her a smile that he no doubt intended to be charming. "I have missed you."

And I have missed you as I would a poisonous rash. "How could you have missed me, sir, when we are barely acquainted?" She lifted her chin defiantly.

He closed his eyes as if her words had wounded him. "How can you say this, Elizabeth? In my heart, I know you very well."

She said nothing. He was toying with her, and she had no desire to play his game.

Keeping his eyes focused on her, the viscount slid from the saddle of his horse, landing gracefully on his feet. Elizabeth backed away, putting more distance between them, but she knew very well she could not outpace him. She was wearing heavy skirts; he could catch her easily. One side of his mouth quirked upward at this sign of her discomfort.

As he stalked toward her, the viscount removed his thick leather riding gloves as if preparing to touch her. "I do not understand you, Elizabeth—"

"I am not *Elizabeth* to you, sir," she said, pleased her voice did not shake.

He shook off this rebuke. "Most women would leap at the chance to be the wife of Viscount Billington."

They would not if they knew your true character, Elizabeth thought darkly. As he continued to advance, Elizabeth shifted sideways, closer to the man's horse.

"I do not believe we would suit." Elizabeth kept her voice light.

He spread his arms wide. "I do not know why you would say that."

Elizabeth edged further from him but kept her eyes on his. "I am just a simply country miss…and you are—"

"A viscount. I know, Elizabeth. But you should not allow that to intimidate you."

"You mistake me, sir," Elizabeth said through gritted teeth. "I intended to say you are a blackguard."

His face turned red, and he lurched toward her. She darted behind his horse, peering around the creature's neck to watch the man. He took a deep breath and spoke slowly as if addressing an unruly child. "It is not as if you have another choice, Elizabeth. After that unfortunate incident at the ball—"

Unfortunate incident! Elizabeth ground her teeth. She knew the event was no accident; there were too many coincidences. The viscount had engineered it all.

"No other man would have you for his wife," he continued.

Elizabeth kept her face carefully blank; she would not give him the satisfaction of knowing that such words found their mark, but she was bleeding inside. Although she had always known that marrying for love was unlikely, the possibility had been a cherished hope. Now she knew that she would never marry—for any reason.

It was still a far better fate than being shackled to this man. "Then I will remain unmarried," she said simply.

His eyebrows shot upward. Was it really so surprising? "Surely marrying me is preferable to a lifetime of loneliness." He frowned; she must have piqued his pride.

She allowed a corner of her mouth to curve upward. "By comparison, a lifetime of loneliness is no deprivation, sir."

Somehow his face grew even redder. "Are you hoping for a bigger marriage settlement? Do not play with me. I know you want to marry me," he growled.

Elizabeth's anger flared. How dare he make such declarations? "I would rather wed your horse."

He advanced, each meaty hand curled into a fist. "You must quit this absurdity and bow to the inevitable. We both know it is only a matter of time."

She shrank back against his horse's flank with no obvious means of escape.

His smile was rather sinister. "You will kiss me. Now."

Elizabeth had already suffered through one kiss with the man and had no desire to repeat the experience. She pressed against the horse, her pulse pounding in her ears. Swallowing, she tried to moisten a mouth as a dry as a desert. Why had she baited him? His eyes gleamed with anger.

When he was a few feet from her, she cast her eye over his shoulder, raising her brows in surprise. "Who could that be?"

As she had hoped, Lord Henry turned to see the newcomer. Elizabeth immediately grabbed hold of his horse's saddle, and putting her foot in the stirrup, she heaved herself onto its back, landing in an ungainly heap.

By the time the viscount turned back to her, she had managed to sit upright, her skirts bunched up around her knees and the reins in her hands. The startled horse was dancing around, making it dangerous for the viscount to come too close. He shouted threats and curses at her.

She dug her heels into the horse's flank, hoping the beast would take commands from someone other than its master. Perhaps she applied too much pressure. The creature took off in a flash, requiring Elizabeth to grab the pommel with one hand to avoid spilling out of the saddle.

Over the thundering of the horse's hooves, the viscount's voice still screamed at her. But soon they were out of earshot. The horse's hooves kicked up dust, and wind whipped her clothing and hair. Her legs, too short for the stirrups, stuck out to the side, revealing far more of her lower leg than was at all proper, and much of her skirt was bunched uncomfortably around her waist. However, when she glanced over her shoulder, the viscount was lost to sight, and Elizabeth allowed herself to relax slightly.

Well, now I have escaped, but what if he accuses me of stealing his horse?

***

Darcy was nearing a bend in the road when he heard the pounding of hooves; a horse was approaching at a fast speed. He reined his mount to the side of the road just in time to avoid a collision with a bay stallion thundering into sight—with Elizabeth Bennet perched improbably on its back. The skirt of her dress was hiked up, and both of her legs were visible to the knee. Darcy could not help noticing how shapely they were.

The horse was a thoroughbred from elite bloodlines, far too fine to belong to her family, and he could not imagine that she would set out for a ride without a proper sidesaddle. Where had she obtained such a creature? Elizabeth was pulling on the reins, and—perhaps because it did not recognize the rider—the stallion had slowed but was not stopping.

Without thinking twice, Darcy spurred his own mount into action, causing it to lurch toward the careening horse as it rounded the bend. Leaning low over the pommel of his saddle, Darcy managed to grab the stallion's reins and pulled back sharply as he yelled commands at the animal.

Darcy doubted that his words had much impact on the beast, but the added drag of another horse's weight on the reins slowed the stallion. He maintained a steady pressure until the horse slowed to a walk and finally stopped altogether. Darcy dismounted, looping the animal's reins around a tree branch, and offered Elizabeth a hand to help her down from the horse.

The hand that clasped his was trembling and moist even through the leather of her glove. She clambered awkwardly down from the saddle and stood on unsteady legs as she smoothed her skirts around her ankles. Her whole body shook. "Are you unharmed, Miss Bennet?" he inquired, running his eyes up and down her form.

She gave a shaky laugh, and Darcy could not help admiring her fortitude. Many women of his acquaintance would have swooned after such an episode. "Yes, I thank you for your timely intervention. I believe the only damage is to my dignity. I assure you that I do not customarily ride a horse like a sack of potatoes."

Darcy blinked. "Undignified" was not one of the adjectives he had thought to apply to the sight of Elizabeth on the back of a horse, particularly not with so much leg revealed. "Of course. I would imagine you are a far superior rider with a proper sidesaddle."

She brushed errant strands of hair from her face. "You are very kind to make such an assumption given the display you just witnessed."

How odd to be discussing Elizabeth's horsemanship when something was so obviously wrong. How had she acquired a horse, and why was she riding at such speeds?

"On the contrary," Darcy returned. "It requires great skill to remain atop a strange horse under such circumstances. I am quite impressed."

She regarded him with narrowed eyes for a moment, as if assessing his sincerity. Finally, she said, "I thank you for the compliment, sir."

Would she think him impertinent to inquire about the circumstances of her ride? But surely the unusual situation cried out for some kind of explanation. "You were in quite a hurry. Is there an emergency?" he asked.

She glanced over her shoulder at the road behind her. "No, I do not believe so."

This ambiguous response left Darcy at something of a loss. Why had she ridden so fast if there was no urgency? And why did she watch the road so intently? Finally, he settled on a different but not unrelated line of inquiry. "I did note that you departed the church on foot."

He had meant his words as a light-hearted jest but cursed himself for a fool when he saw the blood drain from Elizabeth's face. He cleared his throat. "Does, er, the Longbourn stable boast such a creature?" he asked, knowing full well she had not had sufficient time to reach her home.

"No…" Her face was now quite red. "I…er…that is, I—"

"Borrowed the mount?" he inquired as though a simple explanation would work. He reached out and took her gloved hand in his. "Please be assured, Miss Bennet, I only wish to help."

Her eyes widened as if she had not expected such an offer from him, although he could not imagine why. But he was then rewarded with a small smile and a slight loosening of the tension in her shoulders. She let out a long breath. "No, indeed. The horse actually is the property of"—she cleared her throat —"Viscount Billington."

"Billington!" Darcy echoed in surprise, releasing her hand. That was the last name he expected to hear. "He lent you his mount?" Was Darcy wrong in assuming she wished to have no connection with the man?

"He did not precisely loan it to me—" She covered her mouth with her hand. "Although I am quite concerned he could label me a horse thief. I must be sure the beast is returned to him." She pressed her lips together into a white line. "Perhaps I should not have— Oh, what a terrible tangle I have created!"

Suddenly, the various oddly shaped pieces of the puzzle fell into place. He took a step closer to her. "Billington accosted you on the road?" His voice was a low growl.

She nodded miserably but lifted her chin and met his gaze. "The horse was the only way to escape."

To Darcy's own surprise, he began to laugh. "Serves him right! You should keep the animal."

Elizabeth's eyes were wide, and her mouth hung open. Darcy could only imagine the expression on Lord Henry's face when Elizabeth jumped into his horse's saddle. Darcy laughed even harder.

Her brows drew together. "Did you, perhaps, help Mr. Lehigh finish off the communion wine?"

Thinking of the vicar sobered Darcy, and he shook his head. "Miss Bennet, to be clear, I believe you should be commended. A lady should always have a horse at hand when encountering such a man," Darcy said.

Elizabeth's eyes widened. "You heard about—?"

"The incident at the ball? Indeed—"

She backed away from him. "I cannot imagine that what you heard is to my credit, sir. I thank you for your assistance, but I should return home…" Her face turned in the direction of Longbourn.

"There is no need to depart so precipitously," Darcy said.

When she looked back at him, an odd smile played on her lips. "Truthfully, sir, it is best if you are not seen with me. You must understand"—her voice lowered to a whisper —"I have amazing powers of corruption. A single conversation with me about ribbons would be enough to drive an innocent young girl to wantonness." She gave him a conspiratorial smile.

Darcy could not help returning the smile. "I will take my chances."

Elizabeth shook her head, no longer smiling. "No. You should not be seen with me."

"Please, Miss Bennet—" Darcy's hand reached out to her of its own volition.

Elizabeth's eyes focused on his outstretched hand. He cleared his throat. "I…I do not know what others believe about the story, but I…" His hand floated between them, an awkward reminder of the total impropriety of his behavior. He cleared his throat and started again. "I do not know Lord Henry, but I know men like him who use such…tactics to take advantage of innocent women." She continued to regard him with a level gaze. He let his hand drop.

Was she horrified at his presumption? Perhaps he should not have mentioned the incident at all. Such delicate situations were not spoken of in polite company. *I am a fool. Why did I say anything at all? Why did I leave London? I cannot be her knight errant.*

Then he noticed Elizabeth's eyes glistening with unshed tears. *I have made her cry!* He was beginning to regret having risen from bed that morning. *Perhaps it would be best for her if I departed for Pemberley and never returned. Although Derbyshire might not be far enough. Perhaps India.*

Elizabeth swallowed, the pale column of her throat moving convulsively. "Y-you believe me?" Her words were a harsh whisper. "N-no one in Meryton b-believes a word of my story save my Papa and Jane. People I have known all my life think I was the agent of my own ruin, but y-you, a virtual stranger…you believe me?"

Darcy did not see himself as a virtual stranger to Elizabeth Bennet, but now was hardly the time to argue the point. "Yes, I believe you. You would never behave in such a…reckless manner. From what I have heard, it is clear the viscount imposed himself upon you. Almost certainly he arranged the situation with the purpose of compromising your virtue."

If possible, Elizabeth's face grew even paler. "I suspected as much."

Darcy shrugged. "It is possible he believes he harbors affection for you. But I am confident he engineered the scene of your compromise." He cleared his throat. "That is hardly the act of a man who genuinely cares for your wellbeing."

"No," Elizabeth agreed faintly.

Darcy had expected her anger at the man to be more forceful. Was it possible she was wavering in her disdain for him?

He stepped toward her, wishing he dared to take her hand again. "I urge you…I beg of you…do not accept the man's offer!"

She frowned, and her mouth dropped open slightly. Was he too forceful? Too close? He took a few steps backward.

"I assure you, sir, I have not the least intention of accepting his proposal. I would rather remain unmarried my whole life." A muscle twitched in her jaw. Most likely she believed that would be her fate.

He had to disabuse her of that notion. He lurched toward her, intending to take her hand. "Elizabeth, I—"

Her eyes widened at this familiarity, but what he intended to say next was interrupted by the sound of footfalls from behind them. They turned their heads as Lord Henry rounded the bend. Red in the face and sweating profusely, Lord Henry was a bit worse for wear. Upon discovering Elizabeth and Darcy—and his horse—at the side of the road, he trudged to a halt.

Lord Henry straightened his waistcoat and fixed his cravat as he took in the scene before him. "Ah, here is Maximilian. Excellent," the viscount said as if he had momentarily misplaced his horse and was relieved to have the temporary inconvenience resolved. He probably had intended to say something quite different to Elizabeth when he caught up to her, but Darcy's presence confounded him. No doubt he was wondering how much Darcy knew about their situation.

Darcy untied the horse's reins and handed them into Lord Henry's keeping. The other man took them but then simply stood there unmoving. They maintained a silent tableau for several seconds. Darcy wanted to lead Elizabeth away but dared not turn his back on the other man.

The viscount pulled himself up to his full height, a few inches shorter than Darcy, and held out his hand to Elizabeth. "Elizabeth, come away. There are things we must discuss."

"I have said everything that needs saying," Elizabeth responded coolly.

The sound of her Christian name on the man's lips made Darcy bristle. "You may speak in my presence," he said.

Lord Henry made an irritated gesture. "She is my betrothed, Darcy. There are things we must discuss."

Perhaps the viscount believed Elizabeth would not contradict him before witnesses. If so, he did not have a firm grasp on her character.

"I pray you, sir, remind me again when we became betrothed? I recall refusing your offer, and I am quite sure I have not told you otherwise." Elizabeth's eyes flashed as she spoke. "Do you remember our conversation differently?"

The sarcasm was not lost on Lord Henry. His face flushed even redder, and his lips were set in a thin line.

"I have found," Darcy drawled, "that women usually know if they are betrothed."

The viscount scowled at Elizabeth. "I do not believe you have a choice, my dear."

"It is not the practice in England to force women into marriage," Darcy said. "If Miss Bennet does not wish to be betrothed to you, she will not be."

Lord Henry gave Darcy a disdainful look and then glared at Elizabeth. "You have no other options—after what has passed between us."

Darcy's insides curdled at these words. *What had Elizabeth suffered?* But he kept his face carefully blank.

Elizabeth frowned at the man, her hands balled into fists at her sides. "Nothing passed between us save some rather awkward compliments on my beauty and a very unappealing kiss."

The viscount grimaced. "Nobody believes that was all! Your own family scoffed at the idea."

It is interesting, Darcy thought, *that when he is almost alone with Elizabeth, he does not bother to deny her assertion.* Darcy folded his arms over his chest; perhaps that would prevent him from striking the other man. "I believe her," he said forcefully.

Elizabeth's head swung toward Darcy, her lips slightly apart.

Darcy continued, "In my experience, Miss Elizabeth has always been honest to a fault." Elizabeth's jaw dropped as he spoke; did she not expect him to come to her defense? "Further, I have too high an opinion of her judgment to believe she would willingly consort with you."

The viscount was momentarily struck dumb at the insult. Another man might have challenged Darcy to a duel for such a slight, but Lord Henry was a coward. After a minute he regained control, straightening his shoulders with a sneer. "Now I see how it is, Darcy. You want her for yourself. I damaged the goods, and now you hope to purchase them at a reduced price."

The callousness in the other man's words made Darcy's entire body tighten with anger. Surely Lord Henry did not believe that. Surely he did not regard Elizabeth as something to be bought and sold like a bolt of cloth in a milliner's shop! Outrage stopped his throat.

"Well, I won't have it!" Lord Henry declared. "I put forth the effort, and she is now mine for the taking."

Darcy finally found his voice. "I do not have the aspirations to which you allude, sir." His words were excruciatingly polite, but his tone was acid. He advanced on the other man, hoping to intimidate him into departing. "You have insulted me and this lady in every possible way. I suggest you mount your horse and leave before I am forced to take action!" Using his superior height to advantage, he loomed over the viscount, who backed away a few paces.

Lord Henry grasped his horse's reins with a trembling hand, pointing a threatening finger at Darcy. "This is not over, Darcy! She is not yours to have. She is *mine*."

Darcy was astonished at the sound of Elizabeth's laughter. "And here I believed I belong to myself." She tapped a thoughtful finger to her lips. "How in the world could I have been so mistaken?"

The viscount leered at her. "You will be mine! You shall see!" With a quick foot in the stirrup, he flung himself into the saddle, wheeled about his mount, and soon disappeared around the bend.

Only when he was sure the scoundrel was gone did Darcy turn his eyes to Elizabeth. She was frozen in the middle of the road, apparently horrified by these events. "I am sorry you were forced to witness that display of temper and ill manners," he told her, keeping his voice low and calm.

She exhaled a shaky laugh. "Well, sir, you will not find my behavior recommended in a book of lady's manners!"

Darcy grinned despite himself, running a hand through his unruly curls. "I fear Lord Henry does not bring out the best in me."

"You need not apologize to me." She blinked, refocusing her eyes on his face. "He...I...what did he mean? Why did he think you wanted me for yourself?" She gave a little laugh as if the whole notion was absurd.

It broke Darcy's heart. Did she believe herself so unworthy of his attentions? He scrubbed his face with one hand, trying to think how to phrase it delicately. His father's instructions on a gentleman's conduct had never addressed how to converse with a lady on such a prurient subject. "I deduce from your statements that Lord Henry attempted— unsuccessfully—to compromise your virtue and then made it appear that he had?"

Elizabeth nodded mutely.

"I do not believe he did so with the intention of marrying you."

A line formed between her brows. "But you said you believed he had tricked me—"

"He undoubtedly wished you to fall into his clutches. But once there, marriage is not his aim."

"He made me an offer—"

"A promise he has no intention of fulfilling. I do not believe the viscount's family is particularly well-heeled. He needs a rich wife."

Her hand flew to her mouth. "He would not marry me at all?" she whispered in horror.

Darcy grimaced, hating to be the one to force her to see such ugliness. "It has been done before by unscrupulous men. He compromises your virtue, or makes everyone believe he has done so, until you have no recourse but to accept him. He would take you back to his estate with the promise of marriage, but the ceremony would never happen. Once there, you would be completely within his power. In such a way an unscrupulous man can force a woman to become his mistress."

For a moment she appeared about to cast up her accounts. "I had not thought him as bad as all that," she whispered. Darcy experienced the desire to apologize on behalf of his entire sex. "And he thought," Elizabeth continued, "that you—?"

Darcy nodded grimly. "He thought I was interceding to steal his 'prize' at the last minute. But I assure you, Miss Elizabeth, I would never—"

"No, of course not," Elizabeth said hastily as if the words were too awful to be uttered aloud. "You are an honorable man."

Her simple statement brought Darcy an inordinate amount of pleasure. He fought the impulse to blurt out an offer of marriage on the spot. Elizabeth was shaken and disturbed by the viscount's behavior and still seemed uneasy about Darcy's presence. It was neither the time nor the place.

Still, he could not help envisioning Elizabeth's surprise and joy when he made the offer. It would solve all of her problems. What a satisfying thought.

"Miss Elizabeth," he asked, "will you permit me to escort you back to Longbourn? I would like to ensure you reach your home without further incident."

Her mouth opened slightly as her eyes met his, and Darcy was seized by a fierce desire to taste her lips.

No. Now is not the time. He forced his eyes to focus on her hands.

"I…yes, I thank you, Mr. Darcy. And thank you for all of your assistance this day."

"It was my pleasure, Miss Elizabeth." Darcy took his horse's reins in one hand and offered her his other arm. And it was thus that they strolled back to her home.

Chapter Six

Mr. Darcy's initial behavior on the road at first convinced Elizabeth that he had an identical twin—or perhaps the faeries had replaced him with a changeling. She would have expected a stiff, formal greeting, and perhaps not even that given what he knew of her disgrace. How had he suddenly transformed into this caring man?

So few people credited her story of the incident at the ball that Elizabeth had all but given up recounting it, yet Mr. Darcy believed her without even hearing the complete story. Was Lord Henry correct that Mr. Darcy hoped to gain some advantage over her through a facade of solicitude? But for what purpose? Mr. Darcy could not possibly want her for his mistress. The thought was absurd.

The disdainful, masterful Mr. Darcy who had stood up to Lord Henry was much closer to the man Elizabeth remembered. But once the viscount was banished, the master of Pemberley regained his pleasant concern for her wellbeing. She could not account for the sudden alteration. If anything, news of her disgrace should make him eschew her company—even avoid all of Hertfordshire. She was entirely puzzled by his behavior but could think of no discreet way to inquire about his change of heart.

For the first time Elizabeth found herself doubting the accuracy of Mr. Wickham's account of Mr. Darcy's character. Perhaps she had been overly hasty in accepting the militia officer's version of events. Mr. Wickham, like the rest of the militia, had avoided the company of the Bennet family since the scandal. Elizabeth was not surprised at the defection, but it contrasted sharply with Mr. Darcy's behavior. Now she wondered if she had judged him too quickly. *I certainly was wrong in guessing which of my friends would stand by me in the face of adversity*, she thought bitterly. *What is one more error in judgment by comparison?*

Long periods of silence characterized their walk, but when Elizabeth struck up a subject of conversation, Mr. Darcy was quite amiable. They discussed the weather, the latest news from the war on the peninsula, and the activities of mutual acquaintances. He was uncharacteristically vague about his purpose in returning to Hertfordshire, saying only that he needed a respite from Town.

Finally, she felt she must say something on the subject which hung heavily in the air between them. "Allow me to thank you again for defending me from Lord Henry."

"No thanks are necessary," he murmured. "It was the right thing to do."

"Many others would not have done so," she said. "In fact, I daresay, *most*. My honor has suffered a severe setback recently." She attempted to keep her tone light. Having rescued her, Mr. Darcy did not deserve to be subject to fretful complaints.

"Not your honor, rather your reputation." The words were so low that Elizabeth strained her ears to hear them.

"I beg your pardon?" she asked, now thoroughly confused. "What is the difference?"

He frowned at her, his mouth set in a grim line, but Elizabeth refused to be deterred. She was beginning to suspect that Mr. Darcy's bark was worse than his bite. "I pray you, explain your meaning."

He considered for a moment as they continued to walk. "This is a distinction my father once made to me. Honor is what you know about yourself. Reputation is what others know about you, or believe they know." He cleared his throat. "The people of Meryton think they know what happened between you and Lord Henry. Thus, your reputation has suffered. But *you* know you did nothing wrong; your honor has not been compromised."

He regarded her with unnerving intensity, awaiting her response. She was quite overwhelmed by an intense wave of relief. At least one person understood! And that person believed her honor was intact. Still… "I was gullible," she said slowly.

"That does not compromise your honor." His voice was firm. "Only actions signify. Did you do or say something that would have led Lord Henry to believe you would welcome his advances?"

Her answer was instantaneous. "No! I do not even like the man. I had no desire to accompany him anywhere, including the drawing room at Lucas Lodge."

Did Mr. Darcy's shoulders seem to relax a bit? "If your conscience is clear, your honor is intact," he said simply.

It was amazing how such words could make Elizabeth feel lighter, as if a weighty burden had been lifted from her shoulders. Nothing about her situation had changed, yet it was a little more bearable.

She had been silent a long while and became aware that Mr. Darcy was watching her anxiously. "Forgive me if I have overstepped my bounds," he said.

"Not at all," Elizabeth reassured him. "I am merely contemplating what you have said. Your words have eased my spirit. I thank you."

He shrugged uneasily as if uncomfortable with the praise. "I have often found it useful to remember his words."

They fell into a companionable silence and did not speak again until they neared Longbourn. They crested a small rise, and her home was within sight. Elizabeth had been debating with herself for the last five minutes and finally decided to speak, stopping at the top of the rise and facing Mr. Darcy. "Forgive my impertinence, sir, but I must confess I did not expect such…understanding from you. Your behavior upon the previous visit did not suggest you were interested in a closer friendship with the Bennet family."

His eyes widened. Was she being too frank with him? "I…er…" He removed his hat briefly and ran his fingers through his dark curls. "I apologize if I gave you the impression upon my earlier visit that I did not…care about…your family."

He paused. She said nothing, merely watched him expectantly.

He swallowed. "The truth is…I am most concerned about your wellbeing. I heard about your situation from some mutual acquaintances and"—he stared down at Longbourn, his mouth a thin, firm line —"it recalled to me an experience of my sister's."

Elizabeth's hand covered her mouth. She was horrified at the thought that anyone would experience what she was going through.

"A…friend of the family prevailed upon her to elope with him, but he was only after her dowry. I arrived in time to thwart his plan. But the situation easily could have been far worse for our family." His eyes looked past her, staring at nothing. "Fortunately, nobody knows about her indiscretion, but if it were widely known how much time they spent together unchaperoned, she would be expected to marry the blackguard, which would have made her life miserable."

She had drawn closer to Mr. Darcy without realizing it. "I am so sorry. She is very young, is she not?"

"Fifteen years of age when it occurred."

"How horrible! Your poor sister." What she must have suffered!

Mr. Darcy shrugged. "The worst did not come to pass. But Georgiana and I both learned how fragile a woman's reputation can be."

Elizabeth nodded, considering what he had said. "I appreciate your sympathy, sir." Her words were stiff and formal, but how could it be otherwise with a man she knew so little?

Mr. Darcy again offered his arm, and they resumed their walk in silence. But after a minute, Mr. Darcy cleared his throat. "I...um...felt the need to tell you the story for another reason."

"Oh?"

He took a deep breath. "The young man who caused Georgiana so much heartache was George Wickham."

Elizabeth could not prevent a sharp intake of breath. She never would have expected such behavior from the charming young man, but as she considered it, various pieces of the story fitted together. Mr. Darcy's dislike of the man. Mr. Wickham's avoidance of his childhood friend. And the militia officer's loss of interest in Elizabeth when scandal struck.

"That is unexpected news," she said finally. "But thank you for telling me."

Her companion nodded. "I never would have forgiven myself if Wickham had taken advantage of you—or someone close to you."

They crossed the remaining distance to Longbourn in silence. As they grew closer to her home, Elizabeth experienced a sense of increasing dread. Under ordinary circumstances, she would invite Mr. Darcy into the drawing room for some tea and conversation with her family. However, these circumstances were far beyond ordinary, and she feared her mother's reaction upon seeing her with the man. Mrs. Bennet had always disliked Mr. Darcy, and she was barely civil to Elizabeth these days. *How would she react to seeing us together? No, it would not be good. Perhaps I can claim a headache and bid him goodbye before reaching the front door.*

As they rounded a bend in the road near Longbourn, Elizabeth disengaged her hand from Mr. Darcy's arm, rather more reluctantly than she would have expected. It felt unaccountably natural there. She turned to Mr. Darcy with words about a headache on her lips; however, before she could open her mouth, a shriek emanated from the direction of Longbourn.

"Lizzy! Lizzy!" Elizabeth turned to see her mother, hands bunched in her skirts, rushing toward them. A coach and driver waited outside Longbourn's entrance. Presumably her mother had been about to embark on an outing when she spied them. What horrid luck!

Her mother stumbled to a stop in front of her, puffing and out of breath. "Lizzy! What on earth is the matter with you?" She gestured wildly at her daughter, apparently oblivious to Mr. Darcy's presence. "Your hair! Your clothes! You look as if you have been tramping through the woods. What have you been getting into now? What if someone should see you?"

Elizabeth felt her face heat, no doubt turning all shades of red. She did not even know whether she was more embarrassed by the rebuke or her mother's lack of decorum.

"Indeed, madam," Mr. Darcy intoned. "It is almost as if she had been rushing about the countryside shrieking loudly."

Mrs. Bennet turned to Mr. Darcy and blinked at him, not comprehending his sarcasm.

The situation likely was unsalvageable, but Elizabeth fell back on her manners anyway. She gestured to Mr. Darcy. "Mama, you may remember Mr. Darcy?"

Her mother's mouth formed a perfectly round "o" of surprise. "Mr. Darcy! Oh! Oh!" She fluttered her hands and then executed an excessively deep and clumsy curtsey which threatened to pitch her into the dirt. "What has Lizzy been about this time, sir? Has she been causing you trouble? She is such a sly, headstrong creature!"

Elizabeth had not believed it was possible for her face to get hotter. *I must be as red as a tomato now!*

Mr. Darcy returned the curtsey with a stiff bow; his blank face betrayed neither disgust nor amusement at her mother's behavior. "Indeed, madam, Miss Elizabeth has done nothing wrong." Elizabeth felt a rush of gratitude that he did not mention the horse theft.

Mrs. Bennet took another look at Elizabeth's disheveled state and sniffed loudly in disbelief. "Such a troublesome girl!" she exclaimed. "She is quite a trial to me!" Then her face lit up as it occurred to her that Mr. Darcy's presence was an opportunity. "Why don't you come into the house for a cup of tea, and you can converse with some of my *other* daughters?"

Elizabeth suppressed a desire to roll her eyes. Her mother was not nearly as subtle as she believed.

Mr. Darcy stiffened. "Not today, I thank you. But I will take the opportunity to call another day."

As he mounted his horse, Mrs. Bennet took the opportunity to voice effusive offers of welcome and exclamations over the virtues of Cook's poppy-seed cakes. Before he turned his horse toward Netherfield, Mr. Darcy's gaze caught and held Elizabeth's as if he intended to communicate some important message to her. But it was lost on Elizabeth. Seconds later, he had bidden them farewell and rode away.

Mrs. Bennet's strained smile disappeared immediately. "Well, we shall never see him again," she remarked in a peevish tone. "Only recently returned to the neighborhood, and you have already managed to disaffect him."

That was not what had happened! Or was it? He had been so sympathetic…yet he had abandoned her at the first opportunity. Perhaps he, like all the others, did not want to be seen in her company.

"He said he would call another day, Mama," Elizabeth pointed out.

Her mother waved this away. "Stuff and nonsense! He was merely being polite. He could hardly wait to depart." She emitted a long-suffering sigh. "Not that it means anything to *you*, but he might have shown an interest in one of your sisters."

"I thought you did not care for Mr. Darcy," Elizabeth reminded her.

Mrs. Bennet scowled at her daughter. "That was *before*. Now we must take any port in a storm. I will be well pleased if *any* of my daughters makes a reasonably good match."

Elizabeth sighed. Her mother never failed to remind her how her disgrace affected the family. She might love Elizabeth, but she hated the scandal her second daughter had visited upon them—a disgrace which Elizabeth had compounded by refusing to take the only action that would silence the rumors: accepting the viscount's offer. Lord Henry was rich, well-spoken, and had a good family name; most of Meryton was charmed by him. Mrs. Bennet could not understand why Elizabeth did not leap at the opportunity to marry him.

Her mother sniffed again, turned on her heel, and stalked toward the waiting carriage. Elizabeth trudged toward Longbourn with far less alacrity.

Elizabeth reminded herself of Mr. Darcy's words about the viscount. It was a comfort to know the master of Pemberley believed she was doing the right thing.

How grateful she now was that she had listened to her own misgivings and not yielded to Lord Henry's importuning. Yet it was a rather cold comfort. She doubted her mother would believe her even if she repeated Mr. Darcy's words. And despite her words to her mother, Elizabeth rather doubted that Mr. Darcy would visit again. He had departed with such haste that the very air around Longbourn might have been tainted.

I shall never see him again, she thought, unable to express why the thought made her sad. She turned and looked back at the road, but any sign of his passage was long gone.

***

Darcy did not sleep well, and the next morning he was up and dressed well before the dawn. Leaving Elizabeth at Longbourn, in the company of her hostile mother, had been one of the most difficult things he had ever done. Now her proximity was impossible to forget. Knowing that Elizabeth was a mere three miles away…the need to see her was like a fever in his blood.

Despite the unpleasantness the day before, just being in her presence had been a joy. She was as lovely as ever, and the conversation between them had been interesting and lively. She had not smiled much on the previous day, but Darcy could recall what a glorious sight it was. He could not wait for a day when he would be the recipient of such smiles. *I will soon chase away the shadows of sorrow in her eyes.*

He had determined that he would make the offer today. Although it might be more seemly to wait until he had been in Hertfordshire longer, he could not stand the thought of her suffering one more day when he could lift her burden. However, thoughts about the proposal itself provoked clammy palms and a stomach which tied itself in knots. He had no doubt about the outcome, but it was hard to escape the knowledge that his life was about to change.

In the early morning light, he meandered the halls of Netherfield, driving the staff to distraction. Finally, the hour was late enough to make an early morning call on the family at Longbourn. Having had plenty of time to devise his strategy, Darcy took Bingley's phaeton rather than ride horseback.

The phaeton's bench was not as high as some, but it was still a dashing vehicle: lightweight and agile—a pleasure to drive. Darcy reached Longbourn faster than ever before.

His arrival threw the Bennet household into a frenzy, which puzzled him exceedingly. On the previous day he had indicated that he would return for a visit. However, it appeared that nobody had anticipated such an early visitor, and many of the household were not prepared.

The housekeeper escorted him into the drawing room where he sat alone for a full ten minutes. Then he was joined by the two youngest Bennet girls, whose names he could not recall. They simpered and flirted, but when he did not provide them with the desired response, they fell to discussing Meryton gossip between themselves. Eventually, the room filled with Mrs. Bennet, the middle daughter Mary, and Jane, who seemed as pleasant and unruffled as ever.

Tea and some tasty poppy-seed cakes were brought in. They exchanged pleasantries about the weather, the health of various relatives, and the doings of the Bingley family. Still, Elizabeth did not join them. Darcy was at a bit of a loss as to how he could inquire about her whereabouts without appearing impertinent. It was rather early for a walk or a visit to another household. Was she sick? The thought made his insides grow cold.

Darcy chewed a cake while listening to Mrs. Bennet's account of the trembling in her left leg. Richard would know how to discreetly raise the subject of Elizabeth; even Bingley might manage it, but Darcy was always tongue-tied and awkward in such situations.

The two younger girls—one of whom was named Lydia, but he could not remember which—were arguing about whose embroidery stitching was better. "Denny said my stitching was the most uniform he ever set eyes on!" the taller of the two girls exclaimed.

The darker-haired one retorted, "Mama said the handkerchief I gave her was the nicest pattern she had ever seen! Didn't you, Mama?"

Mrs. Bennet waved her hands about. "I do not know what I said! But both of these girls are quite accomplished, are they not, Mr. Darcy?"

Darcy startled, having no desire to be drawn into such a conversation. "Indeed. Their embroidery—what I see of it—is quite fine," he ventured.

There was a lull in the conversation. Had he said something wrong? Again? Was that not the way this game was played? Empty compliments were the stock in trade of a visitor to a family's home.

Oh. The two younger sisters had locked eyes. "Mr. Darcy likes my embroidery best!" the taller girl taunted her sister.

"You haven't even shown it to him yet!" the other one cried.

Darcy pinched the bridge of his nose. How long had he been there? Two days?

The shorter girl continued, "My stitches might not be completely even, but they are quite good…well, adequate. At least they are better than Lizzy's—" She abruptly clapped her hand over her mouth, her eyes darting to her mother.

The air was suddenly sucked from the room as all the sisters froze in place. The younger girls stared apprehensively at their mother while Jane seemed to implore Mrs. Bennet with her eyes. The older woman's lips were pursed tightly, and she practically quivered with emotion. Had Darcy not been present, no doubt the younger girls would be experiencing quite a dressing down.

Nevertheless, he was puzzled by the air of tension. It was not a secret that they had a fifth sister. Was she so out-of-favor that they could not even mention her name? Perhaps Darcy could take this opportunity to learn something.

"Where is Miss Elizabeth? I had such a pleasant conversation with her yesterday," he said.

Mrs. Bennet blinked, fiddling nervously with the necklaces on her capacious chest. "Lizzy? Lizzy?" she echoed as if only now recalling that she had another daughter. She waved a lace handkerchief. "She is around somewhere. I cannot say that I know."

Surely he could be more forceful in making his desire for her company known. He considered how to construct such a request.

Fortunately, Jane Bennet saved him the trouble by rising and saying, "I will find Lizzy." Nobody could have failed to notice the glare Mrs. Bennet aimed at her eldest daughter as she slipped out of the room. Darcy's heart ached for Elizabeth, ostracized even within her own family.

Mrs. Bennet maintained continuous conversation about rosettes on shoes, but it finally stuttered to a halt when Jane returned with Elizabeth in tow.

Elizabeth always took Darcy's breath away, but today it was more out of concern than admiration. While yesterday she had been wind-blown and ruddy, today she was pale and solemn with none of her usual animation. She curtseyed properly to Darcy, and he returned a bow, but she said nothing and did not meet his eyes.

Darcy previously had noticed that Elizabeth's ordeal was taking its toll upon her; she had lost weight, and there were dark shadows under her eyes. But somehow she was even more subdued following a night in her family's house than after an encounter with Lord Henry. Darcy wanted to rail against Mrs. Bennet and any of the sisters who made his Elizabeth feel unworthy. If only he could scoop her into his arms and carry her away to Pemberley that instant!

The conversation proceeded upon its halting course, including such animating subjects as the weather, that year's crop yields, shoe rosettes (again), long sleeves, the shocking disarray of Mrs. Long's wardrobe, the weather (again), how long the militia might stay in Meryton, and, yet again, the weather.

Darcy dug his fingernails into the palms of his hands—and endured.

Elizabeth said not a word. On one occasion she seemed about to speak, but her mother gave her a sharp look and she subsided. Darcy thought about directing a comment or question to her specifically but feared he would make her situation worse.

Finally, the bounds of Darcy's politeness had been exceeded. An escape from the overheated room was necessary, not only for his own sake but also for Elizabeth's. When the conversation stuttered to a stop, he announced, "I have the good fortune to have Bingley's phaeton with me today and thought I would take it out to see the horses run their paces." The two younger girls ceased bickering about bonnet ribbons and regarded him with great interest. One emitted a high-pitched squeal.

"Unfortunately," Darcy continued, "I only have space for one other party. Miss Elizabeth, would you do me the honor?"

Her head, bent over her stitching, swung up immediately, and she regarded him with an astonished—almost horrified—expression.

Mrs. Bennet was equally astonished and far more horrified. She drew breath to voice her opinion, but Darcy spoke before her. "Unless you have any objection, Mrs. Bennet?"

He had neatly forestalled her criticism. "Ah…no…that is, of course not. Any of my daughters is at your disposal." She blinked rapidly and then hastily added, "For a ride in the phaeton."

"Excellent." He glanced at Elizabeth, who nodded, a dazed expression on her face. Darcy rose and held out a hand to her. She stood slowly and laid her fingers in his hand as if she were touching a live snake. But he was able to draw her into the hallway, whereupon she said in a low voice, "I must gather my pelisse." Darcy released her hand and strode toward the front entrance to retrieve his greatcoat, subduing his elation. She would soon be his!

Chapter Seven

Elizabeth stood by the back door, struggling into her pelisse. *I should take it to the front hallway; Mr. Darcy is enough of a gentleman that he would help me don it.*

She was unsurprised when her mother appeared. "Well, Lizzy, you have been given quite an honor, though you scarcely deserve it."

Saying nothing, Elizabeth continued to button her pelisse.

"A ride on Mr. Darcy's phaeton is wasted on you!" her mother declared. "He cannot possibly have good intentions toward a woman with such a tarnished reputation." Elizabeth hid her wince as she draped a shawl around her shoulders. "And you are practically betrothed."

"I am not betrothed," Elizabeth hissed.

Her mother waved away this objection. "You will see reason eventually. My point is, you would do better by this family if you gave up the ride with Mr. Darcy altogether. You could tell him you are suddenly indisposed and suggest that he take Lydia or Jane instead." Mrs. Bennet smiled winningly, her hands folded across her stomach, as if this were the best solution for everyone involved.

"Mama," Elizabeth said, "he does not wish to ride with Jane or Lydia. He asked me specifically."

"You cannot be so selfish as to deny your sisters such an opportunity!" her mother cried.

Elizabeth sighed. Perhaps she was being a bad sister by not encouraging his interest in another Bennet daughter. But a ride in a phaeton sounded so lovely after being confined at home for so long. "Mr. Darcy has made the request. We might anger him if we do not honor it."

"Well"—her mother pursed her lips —"I suppose there is no harm in satisfying his momentary whim. Perhaps he will take Lydia out afterward."

Elizabeth did not voice her opinion that Lydia and Mr. Darcy would be a match made in hell.

"And you must take every opportunity to tell him how Jane is sought after by all the men in Hertfordshire."

"I will only say nice words about Jane," Elizabeth promised, knowing full well that Mr. Darcy had no desire to discuss the woman his best friend had been courting.

"Very well." Her mother nodded as she talked herself into the scheme. "Do hurry, Lizzy! You do not want to make him wait."

She pushed Elizabeth toward the front of the house, making her stumble and catch the wall for balance. However, as Elizabeth rushed toward the door, her mother's words floated through her mind: he cannot possibly have good intentions toward a woman with such a tarnished reputation. What did Mr. Darcy want with her now that she was disgraced? And what would Elizabeth do if it was something improper? She could not shake the thought as she passed through Longbourn's entrance out into the chilly air.

Mr. Darcy greeted her with a gentle smile that allayed some of her anxiety. But Elizabeth knew all too well the deceit a pleasant smile could hide; even now most inhabitants of Meryton found the viscount quite charming. Of course, Mr. Darcy had never taken the effort to make himself well-liked, by Elizabeth or anyone else in Meryton. It was actually an obscurely comforting thought.

Taking her hand, Mr. Darcy helped her onto the bench of the phaeton. It was not as high as some high-perch phaetons, but it certainly was the highest bench Elizabeth had ever occupied. The effect was slightly alarming; the ground was as far away as if she had climbed to the top of a tree, and the springs under the bench caused it to sway precariously with the slightest motion. One of the horses snorted, and the phaeton rolled forward an inch; Elizabeth grabbed her seat with some distress. On the whole, I would prefer a tree.

Mr. Darcy climbed up on the other side of the bench, which seemed far too small for two people. His hip brushed hers as he seated himself, and a blush warmed Elizabeth's cheeks. He took the ribbons into his hands, and the horses leapt forward as if they had been waiting impatiently for the chance to run.

Elizabeth clutched her seat and prayed that her bonnet ribbons were tied securely. Wind whipped around her, brushing back the few curls that had escaped the bonnet. The February air was mild, but their speed created a breeze that chilled her face and reddened her cheeks.

Once Elizabeth had accustomed herself to the sensations, however, they were quite exhilarating. The familiar sights along the road raced past in a blur of brown and green. She never had traveled so quickly in her life. When the phaeton shot around a curve in the road, it almost felt like flying.

Elizabeth could not help it. A laugh bubbled up from inside and through her lips, provoking a sidelong glance and a half smile from her companion. Then he snapped the reins, urging the horses to even faster speeds, although it hardly seemed possible.

Elizabeth's bonnet ribbons whipped around in the wind, and her clothing was plastered against her body. Still, she could not prevent another laugh. Who would have imagined a simple carriage ride could be so thrilling?

Incredibly, her reaction seemed to please Mr. Darcy. Even as he kept his eyes on the road, a smile crept over his lips.

Finally, he reined in the horses to a trot—albeit a far faster trot than Elizabeth was accustomed to. They were on the outskirts of Meryton. How had they arrived here so quickly? Mr. Darcy guided the horses onto Main Street, setting a brisk walking pace that would help them traverse the town without presenting a danger to the people in the street.

Upturned faces followed the phaeton's progress, and hands pointed to it. Eyes widened as they recognized Elizabeth. They were causing quite a stir. No doubt many dinner tables that night would be dominated by conversation about "Mr. Darcy in the phaeton with Elizabeth Bennet." At least for today, she would be known for something other than scandal; everyone would know that at least one person did not mind being seen with her.

Mr. Darcy appeared to be oblivious to the attention. Staring straight ahead, he focused on guiding the horses through the streets. However, his actions were not random, Elizabeth realized. The phaeton easily could have taken the road that led around—rather than through—Meryton, but Mr. Darcy wanted the good people of Meryton to notice her perched next to one of the wealthiest men Hertfordshire had ever seen. Why was he going to such trouble? It must be because he remembered his sister's suffering; he wanted to diminish the effect of the scandal.

It was hard to fathom that this was the same man who had loudly declared her inability to tempt him.

They continued at this sedate pace until they were through the town. Then the phaeton's pace increased, although it did not reach the previous speed. Elizabeth was surprised when Mr. Darcy pulled the phaeton up to a pathway she knew very well.

"You once recommended the walk to Oakham Mount as providing the best views in the neighborhood," Mr. Darcy said. "I was hoping you would show it to me."

"Indeed, it is very fine," Elizabeth responded. Was this the reason for the entire trip? But surely he did not need a guide to Oakham Mount! The way was straight and easy. The man beside her, on the other hand, was complicated and mysterious.

Mr. Darcy climbed down from the high seat and crossed to her side of the vehicle. Elizabeth regarded him dubiously; the ground was very far away, and she saw no way to descend gracefully. Rather than offering her a hand, Mr. Darcy placed one hand on either side of her waist and swung her out of the seat.

Elizabeth's breath caught. It was almost like soaring high on a swing, yet Mr. Darcy's hands on her waist were unexpectedly pleasant. The pressure of his fingers was warm and firm through her dress, lingering for a moment even after she was on solid ground. How odd that she missed the warmth when he released her.

His eyes lingered on her face for a few moments, his expression inscrutable. A prickle of uneasiness crept down Elizabeth's spine. What if Mr. Darcy's motives were not honorable? He himself had pointed out how Lord Henry might scheme to take her virtue without marrying her. Had Mr. Darcy returned to Netherfield last night and decided Elizabeth's disgrace might allow him improper liberties? Had his warning about the viscount been intended to disarm her?

He turned toward Oakham Mount and attacked the path with a determined stride, his long coat swinging behind him. She hurried after him, wishing that there were more people visiting the mount, but on this February morning they were completely alone.

He had defended her from Lord Henry, and he had been very careful with her when she had nearly fallen off the horse—and he was Mr. Bingley's friend. He had done and said nothing to suggest he was untrustworthy. Thus reassured, Elizabeth lengthened her stride, determined to catch up to Mr. Darcy.

The day was not terribly chilly, more like an early autumn day than mid-February. The surrounding fields were fallow, and much of the grass was brown. The pine trees that lined both sides of the pathway were vibrant spots of green against the winter-gray fields. The sun bathed everything in a warm, golden glow.

Despite its name, Oakham Mount was more of a tall hill. But it was a vigorous walk, and Elizabeth was warm and breathing fast when she reached the top a few moments after Mr. Darcy.

He surveyed the view, which was particularly lovely on this clear, sunny day. "I can understand why you venture up here, Miss Elizabeth," he exclaimed. "It presents a very fine picture."

On the left, a cluster of roofs indicated the town of Meryton, a miniature doll village at this distance. Mr. Darcy's eyes traced the route they had just followed. "Is that Longbourn, then?" he asked, pointing.

"Indeed!" she agreed. "It looks very small, does it not?" She shaded her eyes with one hand and pointed with the other. "If you look further down the road, there is a cluster of trees and perhaps a bit of a roof visible. That is Netherfield."

"So it is." Mr. Darcy nodded. He was quiet for another minute, taking in the expanse before them.

"Up here my troubles seem very insignificant. The world does not care about gossip or my reputation," Elizabeth mused. "It is somewhat reassuring actually."

When he finally turned his face to her, she expected an inquiry about whether she was ready to descend. Instead, he said, "You are quite significant to me."

The somber expression on his face set her stomach churning with anxiety. Why had his mood suddenly turned so serious? "Elizabeth, there is another reason I requested your company today," he said, taking one of her hands in his.

The sound of her unadorned name nearly sent her fleeing. Was he about to steal a kiss, like the viscount? Or worse? She held herself very still, wondering if she should run. Others might hold her virtue cheap, but she did not.

The look on his face was almost pained. "In vain I have struggled. It will not do. You must allow me to tell you how ardently I admire and love you."

Now, when she needed to fly, her feet had sunk roots into the ground. Lord Henry also had claimed—in an off-handed way—to love her. And now…Mr. Darcy—who had seemed an ally, if not a friend, yesterday—had revealed himself to be another of the viscount's ilk.

She needed to back away from him and find the path down the hill. She could walk home to Longbourn. If only her feet would move.

His expression had darkened as though the feelings he expressed were unpleasant even for him. "I have sought at every moment to find relief from these feelings that torment me, but to no avail."

He…what? For a moment Elizabeth stopped considering how to escape.

He cleared his throat. "The situation of your family and the total want of propriety of some of your relatives stayed my tongue when I might have declared myself earlier—"

Elizabeth had been the recipient of two other offers of marriage, neither of which had been under the most romantic circumstances. Yet she was fairly certain that insulting the prospective bride's family was not part of the accepted form.

He gazed earnestly into her eyes. "But we can have a small, quick wedding, and I will take you off to Pemberley—where we need not see your family so…frequently."

Elizabeth covered her mouth, stifling an inappropriate laugh, equal parts amusement and relief. A man who sought only to take advantage of her virtue would flatter her to the heavens rather than criticize her family. How odd that Mr. Darcy's lack of tact revealed his sincerity. It must be love.

She struggled to understand him in light of this revelation. Mr. Darcy loves me. He wants to marry me. No, it still did not make sense.

Mr. Darcy was still speaking. "If I had made you an offer at the Netherfield ball, you might have been spared the unpleasantness with Lord Henry."

"Y-you considered proposing then?" Elizabeth asked. This could not be! Until yesterday she believed he violently disliked her. She had been as wrong in her assessment of his character as she had been about Lord Henry. Who else had she misjudged?

"Yes." His lips pressed so tightly together that they turned white. "I have been berating myself for that failure ever since I learned of the viscount's assault on your virtue."

Elizabeth was still having difficulty believing his words. Mr. Darcy had been secretly in love with her the whole time? It was as if her father's horse opened his mouth to speak perfect English.

"Can you forgive me?" he asked, his brows knit together in worry.

The question was so unexpected that it was almost absurd. "There is nothing to forgive, sir. You are not responsible for another man's actions."

"But I might have spared you that trial if I had spoken what was in my heart. Instead, I allowed my disgust over your family's impropriety to blind me to what was important." Hopefully the pinched expression on his face reflected his self-loathing and not his distaste for the Bennets.

Elizabeth clenched her teeth together lest she make a hasty and ill-considered remark. Her family had not been her best advocates recently, but they did not deserve such blanket condemnation.

He is paying me a great compliment, she reminded herself. Anger is not the appropriate response.

His hand clutched hers quite tightly. "So I must make amends now and do what I should have done months ago. Elizabeth Bennet, will you do me the honor of becoming my wife?" He did not smile, but his eyes were wide with hope as he gazed at her.

A variety of emotions tangled together in Elizabeth's mind as she listened to Mr. Darcy's declaration, but her response had never been in doubt.

Her eyes dropped down to focus on their intertwined hands. "I-I thank you for the honor of your addresses, sir. I am very much aware of the compliment you have paid me. But I cannot accept your offer."

Would he be crushed? Angry? She raised her eyes to his face. He could not have looked more surprised if she had handed him a live frog. His mouth was agape, and his eyebrows were climbing up his forehead. Had it not occurred to him that she might decline?

She rushed to explain. "My name has been fatally besmirched, Mr. Darcy. I have resigned myself to the knowledge that my reputation will not recover." Tears threatened, and she blinked them back. She had done enough weeping over her fate. "I could not allow you to join me in my disgrace."

His entire face softened, and he stepped forward, taking her other hand in his. To a distant observer, they would appear very much like a couple pledging their love. "But marrying me will help restore your reputation."

She managed a wan smile. His faith in the power of his name was endearing. "No, Mr. Darcy. I believe if you were to marry me, it would create a great scandal. Your friends would shun you. Invitations to balls would disappear"

He scowled. "I care nothing for that! I do not need anyone's approbation!"

Elizabeth narrowed her eyes, no longer able to contain her frustration. "No? Then why did you hesitate to make me an offer? Why does my family's position trouble you so?"

He blinked. She had shocked him again. "I…that is"—he swallowed —"my reservations about your family are only natural. Their behavior—"

"—Will only continue to give you cause for embarrassment," Elizabeth interrupted. "That is hardly an auspicious start to a marriage, sir." Gently, she pulled one hand from his grasp.

He watched her hand leave his. "No." His voice was a harsh whisper. "I would never...never be embarrassed by you, Elizabeth."

She shook her head. He might believe that at the moment, but would he feel that way in a year? In five years? A man possessing such pride could not let it go so easily.

"Perhaps not," she retorted. "However, you have a sister, do you not? Who is preparing to come out soon?"

Mr. Darcy curled into himself, his eyes closed, as if she had struck him in the chest with a sword. "I-I do." His voice had lost some of its firmness. "But Georgiana will understand."

He does not quite believe that.

She squeezed his hand briefly and then withdrew her other hand from his grasp. "I cannot allow you to take that chance," she said. "I will not allow you to destroy yourself and your family for my sake."

His shoulders slumped. "I beg you to reconsider."

Some of her anger melted in the face of his anguish. She had no wish to cause him pain, but accepting his offer would create far more heartache. What if he only fancied himself in love with her—it was a recent development after all— and changed his mind in two years? He would resent her for having ruined his life—and probably his sister's as well.

She shook her head, hoping her expression was determined. "I am sorry to cause you distress, but this is what must be. Someday you will meet the woman destined to be your bride, and you will be grateful for this moment." She swallowed and glanced away, focusing on the view.

"Do not say such things, Elizabeth." His voice was quite hoarse. "I have never experienced such feelings before."

She clasped her hands together at her waist to prevent shaking. "I am sorry to cause you pain, but I hope it will be of short duration." She still could not look at his anguished face. "I pray you, return me to Longbourn."

He bowed his head, his eyes closed and his lips pressed together tightly. There was a long pause during which she heard nothing save the sounds of his ragged breathing. Then he raised his head to lock eyes with her. "Very well, Miss Elizabeth, but you must understand...I will always be your friend...Always."

***

Darcy closed the front door to Longbourn and walked toward the phaeton as if in a dream. The road and house and sky—everything had a sense of unreality. *Did Elizabeth really decline me? This is not some feverish nightmare?* It was so unexpected that he had trouble fathoming it had happened at all. Not only had she declined his offer, but she had declined it so definitively. She had not demurred and requested time to consider her answer. She had simply told him no.

Her reasons made sense, although Darcy did not see the impediments looming as large as Elizabeth did. Still, she was concerned about ruining his life—and Georgiana's. It was hard to fault that concern.

However, that did not alleviate his anguish one iota.

Black despair hung over him like a dark cloud. His initial horror at Elizabeth's plight had been held in abeyance by the happy scheme of making her an offer. He had assured himself that her suffering would soon be relieved by their marriage. Now that she had prevented him from giving her any assistance, the horror returned full force. She was suffering, and Darcy could do nothing to ameliorate her situation.

However, he was forced to admit that his misery also stemmed from his own sense of loss. He had confidently built a future for himself and Elizabeth since he had decided to propose. He had eagerly anticipated showing her Pemberley, introducing her to Georgiana, sharing comfortable nights before the fireplace, and growing old together. How could he have been so wrong about that future?

He had lost Elizabeth, completely and irrevocably. How was it possible that a future without Elizabeth—in which he married some other woman—was both more likely and far less conceivable? He had allowed himself to hope. Now these treasured dreams lay in pieces.

Elizabeth. His heart mourned.

He did not know how he would make it through the next day, let alone the rest of his life, with the knowledge that she would never be his.

Her objections might not be insuperable, but at the moment Darcy could think of no way to overcome them. As unexpected as her rejection was, her reasons made sense. He had never met a woman—or indeed a person—who was so committed to putting the interests of another ahead of her own. Ironically, it made him love her even more.

Upon entering Longbourn, Elizabeth immediately bade him a solemn goodbye, as if she expected never to lay eyes on him again, and climbed the stairs to her exile. Darcy had watched her go with a lump in his throat, desperately wanting to say something to halt her flight but unable to think of the right words.

Before he could make his escape, however, Darcy had been forced into another hour of increasingly less polite conversation with the Bennets in the drawing room. Mrs. Bennet had added to his distress by practically thrusting Jane Bennet and the youngest sister into his path. Miss Bennet's face had colored with mortification while the younger girl had merely giggled and given him coy glances. Darcy could hardly forgive them of the sin of not being Elizabeth.

How could her own family fail to see her worth?

Having witnessed how they treated Elizabeth before guests, he could only imagine how callously they behaved when they were alone. Elizabeth deserved the opportunity to remove herself from such a situation.

If only there were another way to help her! During the ride back to Longbourn, Darcy tried offering her funds to help her escape from Meryton or the assistance of a solicitor to clear her name. She had declined firmly, observing how improper it would be for her to accept help from him. She was quite right, but Darcy cared more about helping her than he did about propriety.

Even now—with the door closed behind him— he lingered as if a sudden solution to all of Elizabeth's troubles would present itself, or perhaps the woman herself would race out of the door and declare that she had changed her mind about the proposal. He shook his head at his own foolishness and concentrated on placing one foot before the other until he reached the phaeton.

The jingling of a harness and the thudding of hooves warned of an approaching vehicle. A gig rounded the corner at a sedate pace and approached Longbourn's entrance. Darcy winced at the sight of the driver. If he had known such a danger lurked, he never would have lingered near the house.

"Mr. Darcy! I say, Mr. Darcy!" the man called out before the gig ceased moving.

Darcy was of no mood to give consequence to the obsequious man but was not quite churlish enough to ignore someone addressing him by name. Suppressing a groan, he approached the gig. He had recognized the man as his aunt's curate, the one who was related to the Bennets. What was his name?

Darcy searched his memory as he nodded. "…Mr. Collins."

The clergyman almost leapt out of the gig to execute a deep bow. "Mr. Darcy. It is an honor, sir." When Darcy did not respond, the man licked his thin lips and continued. "What a surprise, to see you here! I was unaware of your presence in Hertfordshire, and I would not have expected you to"—he coughed delicately—"associate with the Bennet family."

Instantly, Darcy's shoulders tightened, and he leaned forward—right into Collins's face. "Why is that?" Darcy growled. Were all the clergy in the English countryside so hypocritical?

The other man was nonplussed, taking several steps backward. "Well, surely you have heard…of course, you know about…Miss Elizabeth's unfortunate…journey into sin."

His hands had clenched into fists; Darcy relaxed them very deliberately. It would be unfortunate if he struck a man of the cloth.

Collins continued to prattle on blithely, unaware of his danger. "I thought her waywardness might have been occasioned by a lack of guidance on the part of Mr. and Mrs. Bennet. But from what Mrs. Collins has told me, Miss Elizabeth has always been an obstinate and headstrong girl, so I am inclined to believe she must be naturally bad." He shook his head with completely false sincerity. "Such a blow to the family. Compared to the disgrace they must endure, her death would be a blessing."

Gritting his teeth, Darcy reminded himself forcefully that murder was a crime. Good Lord! The man could provoke the most peace-loving nun to violence! He took two steps closer to the clergyman, a proximity that clearly made the man anxious. "Are you suggesting," he murmured, "that Miss Elizabeth would be better off dead?"

Collins's eyes widened as he accurately assessed Darcy's emotional state. "N-no. N-naturally not. I did not mean to imply such a thing."

Darcy smiled dangerously at the man. "It would be inappropriate to voice such sentiments to anyone in the Bennet family…of course."

Collins swallowed. "O-of course."

It would not do. Darcy could envision the idiot vicar making Elizabeth's life worse by hurling insults and thinly veiled accusations at her. Perhaps Darcy could not improve her situation through marriage, but he might persuade the man to be more circumspect. He stood straighter, taking advantage of his six-inch height difference. "It seems to me that as a clergyman, you would see it as your duty not to judge the sinner. Is that not the province of the Lord?" His words managed to be civil, but he could not keep the growl from his voice.

Collins blinked rapidly, his mouth open slightly. Surely this was not a new idea to him? "B-but," the clergyman finally spluttered, "it is my duty to guide sinners to righteousness."

Darcy nodded slowly as if he were explaining a simple story to a rather dull child. "And how have you undertaken that with Miss Elizabeth?"

Collins looked stricken. "Well...I-I...s-she i-is not a member of my flock!" he objected.

"If you are a priest of the church, then surely all Christians are members of your flock," Darcy responded patiently. Really, this man was too stupid for words. No wonder his Aunt Catherine manipulated him so easily.

Collins swallowed. "I s-suppose."

"I would imagine Lady Catherine would not be pleased to learn you had neglected your priestly duties, particularly regarding a member of your own family," Darcy said with as much sincerity as he could muster. In actuality, Darcy suspected Collins had not informed his patroness of the scandal.

"I am not neglectful," Collins asserted.

Darcy clapped the man on the shoulder, nearly knocking him over. "I am quite pleased to hear that. So you have arrived at Longbourn prepared to show Miss Elizabeth every kindness to guide her on the path of righteousness?"

Collins nodded uncertainly. "Yes...yes, I have."

Darcy took the man's moist hand and shook it. "I will commend you to my aunt for your devotion to duty."

Collins beamed. "You are too kind."

Darcy smiled. Well, Elizabeth might be subject to a lecture on scriptures, but at least she was unlikely to experience accusations of a "naturally bad" temperament.

"I have business I must pursue," Darcy said. He climbed into the high seat of the phaeton. "Good day, Mr. Collins!"

Mr. Collins waved, still looking a little bemused. "Good day, sir!"

Darcy departed Longbourn as quickly as he could.

***

Oh, merciful heavens!

Lydia had informed Elizabeth that she had a visitor but maliciously had not revealed his identity. There, taking the seat so recently occupied by Mr. Darcy, was Mr. Collins. She tried and failed to muster a smile. One of the few good results of her disgrace was that Elizabeth had expected Mr. Collins to remain far from Longbourn for years. Why was he here? Her mother and all of her sisters save Jane, who had been sent to town on an errand, were present in the drawing room. Did they know Mr. Collins's purpose?

"Mr. Collins." Elizabeth curtsied.

He gave her a cursory bow, barely bothering to stand. "Miss Elizabeth." Somehow, merely the way he said her name conveyed extreme disapproval. "I applied to your parents for permission to address you, and they kindly granted it."

Elizabeth drew in a breath. This could not be good.

He leaned forward in his chair as she took a seat near his. "I am aware, of course, of your most unfortunate fall from grace."

He made her sound like the snake in the Garden of Eden. Elizabeth bit her tongue against the temptation of a smart retort.

"But it has been brought to my attention that you may not be naturally predisposed to evil." He uttered the words as though granting her a great favor. In the corner of the room, Kitty and Lydia giggled.

Somewhat disconcerted by their reaction, Mr. Collins drew himself up to his full height. "I flatter myself that I might be of some assistance in helping to guide you back to the path of righteousness." Sitting beside the clergyman, Mary nodded tendentiously.

Elizabeth ground her teeth. "Sir, I never departed from the path of righteous living."

Mr. Collins gasped. "You have fallen further than I thought! You no longer recognize the degree of your sin."

Even her mother looked a little shocked at these harsh words.

Desiring to rid herself of the man as quickly as possible, Elizabeth considered the most expeditious strategy. "Sir, it is very good of you to be concerned with the state of my soul. But as a man of the cloth, do you think you should be exposing yourself to such powerful depravity? Particularly without a wooden stake and holy water at hand?"

Lydia and Kitty giggled more loudly while Mrs. Bennet looked confused, and Mary rolled her eyes.

Mr. Collins, on the other hand, nodded earnestly. "I did not believe such measures were necessary, although I do have several cloves of garlic in my satchel." He placed the leather bag on his lap, unfastened the buckles, and opened the flap. A strong odor wafted across the room.

He pulled several pieces of paper from the satchel. "However, I am so fortunate as to have several pamphlets on hand which should prove instructive." He handed her three neatly folded pieces of paper. The first read, "Are you a fallen woman? How to get up again." The second: "After falling into lust: Avoiding the other deadly sins." And the third: "Why the Good Lord wishes you to abstain from carnal relations."

Elizabeth hastily dropped them on a nearby table lest her hands smell like garlic. Really, the whole conversation was too absurd for words. It was growing increasingly difficult to stifle her laughter.

Mr. Collins interpreted her suppressed giggles as a sign of distress. "I know that seeing these words is disturbing. It is not easy to be confronted with evidence of your sin, but I believe the pamphlets will be a source of comfort. If not now, then perhaps later."

Mary nodded solemnly in agreement, but Kitty and Lydia dissolved into helpless giggles. Her mother, however, watched Elizabeth sharply, clearly expecting gratitude.

Elizabeth swallowed. "I thank you, Mr. Collins. I will read them with all the diligence they deserve."

He smiled sagely. "I pray they will help you see the error of your ways."

I am only guilty of one error.

Mr. Collins started to rise.

"One moment, Cousin," she said.

He raised his eyebrows and settled back into his chair.

"I…was…wondering if you have any other pamphlets that might be helpful to me."

Mrs. Bennet nodded approvingly. Mr. Collins beamed and pulled his satchel into his lap once more. When he opened it, even Mary wrinkled her nose. "I have a great many pamphlets. Here is one on the potential evils of gardening. And this one explains how women who read too many novels will never find a husband. This one is about how sea bathing during Advent can wash away your soul."

"And cause pneumonia," Elizabeth murmured.

Mr. Collins frowned at her in confusion. She cleared her throat. "I am seeking something specific." He nodded eagerly. "Do you have anything on how to avoid the company of unscrupulous men? Or perhaps what to do when a man of high rank maligns your character?"

Her mother's lips pursed with disapproval, but Mr. Collins shook his head, failing to grasp Elizabeth's implications. "I cannot believe there would be much of a call for pamphlets of that sort."

"There should be," Elizabeth opined. "They would be most useful."

Finally, her mother stood, no doubt worried what else her wayward second daughter might say to the clergyman. Standing, Mr. Collins smiled obsequiously at Elizabeth. "I pray you will write to me if you have any questions."

She mustered a smile. "When I see the error of my ways, I will be sure to mention it to you."

Her cousin continued to speak even as Mrs. Bennet escorted him through the doorway. "Wonderful! I await your letter," he said over his shoulder.

Elizabeth frowned at his retreating back. *You shall be waiting a long time.*

Chapter Eight

The day was blustery and cold. Walking down Meryton's Main Street, Elizabeth kept her head down so her bonnet shielded her face from the wind. When she glanced up, she saw Mrs. Long a few yards ahead, crossing the street to avoid her. The woman then passed along the other side of the street without so much as a nod to acknowledge Elizabeth. *It does not matter. I would not want to speak with such a nasty gossip anyway.*

Elizabeth hastened her already brisk pace. The snub was a tangible reminder of why her mother hated sending her second daughter to town. Lately Mrs. Bennet even hinted that God would not mind if Elizabeth avoided Sunday services. Although Elizabeth would not miss Mr. Lehigh's sermons, she did not know how she would bear being even more confined to Longbourn.

Her parents had sent her to Meryton out of desperation. Lydia had been gone for many hours, and her father—who had grown more circumspect about his daughters' behavior since Elizabeth's disgrace—had become increasingly anxious. Jane and Mary were both out of the house, and Kitty could not be trusted on any errand involving the youngest Bennet sister. So Mr. Bennet asked Elizabeth if she would find Lydia and bring her home.

Without much difficulty, Elizabeth located Lydia in Colonel Forster's drawing room, giggling with Mrs. Forster and several officers. However, when she had drawn her sister outside for a conversation, the youngest Bennet refused to return home. After whining and pouting, Lydia informed Elizabeth—with a smirk—that a disgraced older sister had no authority to give her orders. All of Elizabeth's arguments about the importance of reputation had been met by raised eyebrows and giggles.

Telling herself it did not matter, Elizabeth was returning to Longbourn in hopes of persuading their father to visit the Forsters and exert *his* authority. He would be extremely displeased at the news. She had never dreamed that Lydia would be so openly defiant.

Lydia is just a silly girl; her opinion matters naught.

Elizabeth brushed some wetness from her eye with a gloved finger. It was one thing to endure such treatment from acquaintances in town and quite another when it came from your own family.

People stared as she walked past. In front of the milliner's shop, three young women laughed behind their fans, giving her sidelong glances. A man in worker's clothing—perhaps a stable hand—did not bother to hide his lascivious admiration of her form. She cringed involuntarily.

Once he passed, she turned her head to watch out of the corner of her eye, ensuring that he had not followed her. Fortunately, he continued on his way, whistling insouciantly. She swallowed hard, willing her tears away. Such treatment would have been unthinkable months ago, but now it was a daily trial.

There was the bookseller's shop on the left. When she last visited the shop a few weeks ago, the owner—once quite friendly to Elizabeth—had given her a haughty glare and asked quite harshly what "she thought she was doing there." Elizabeth had not returned since. She hated her enforced confinement; however, she was beginning to be more charitably inclined toward the thought of never leaving Longbourn again.

Occasionally she fantasized about approaching each individual and explaining the falsity of their assumptions, but she could hardly argue with everyone in the town. *Their opinions do not matter*, she told herself again and again. *I know that my honor is intact.* But with each snub, slight, or rude stare, her soul grew more and more battered. At times she felt so thin and threadbare that there seemed to be hardly anything left of Elizabeth Bennet.

As she had been doing more and more since Mr. Darcy's departure a fortnight ago, Elizabeth conjured up the memory of his face…the light in his eyes as he proposed to her. How could she have doubted his motives? His sincere admiration of her had shone in every smile he directed her way. Despite his insulting words and overweening pride, it was comforting to know that such an honorable man thought her fit to be his wife. He had regarded her with such tenderness, such caring, and she held that image in her heart as a talisman during her darkest days.

There was danger in such memories, however; she could easily start longing for a life that was a mere fantasy. When the yearning for his company grew too great, she recalled Mr. Darcy's arrogant assumption that she would accept his offer despite his complete lack of tact. Even if her disgrace had not stood between them, she reminded herself that his pride surely would have.

Although she encountered nobody else on the road, Elizabeth maintained constant vigilance. By the time she reached the refuge of Longbourn, she was exhausted and trembling. She could almost understand what her mother experienced when she complained about her "poor nerves."

Elizabeth removed her pelisse and bonnet and stopped in her father's study for a quick conversation about Lydia. Then she trudged toward the stairs and the sanctuary of her room. But before she reached the bottom step, her mother's voice floated out from the drawing room. "Lizzy? You have a visitor."

For a moment her heart lifted. Was it possible that one of her friends had braved societal disapproval to visit her? Cassandra Trent? Maybe Marianne Swann? Or perhaps Mr. Darcy had returned? The thought sent her spirits soaring, even though she did not wish him to renew his addresses. She did not. But simply seeing him would warm her heart.

However, all her hopes were dashed when she stepped into the drawing room. Her mother and Jane sat with…Lord Henry.

He regarded her with that lazy smirk she so disliked and a greedy gaze that seemed to devour her with his eyes. Her anger flared. The trembling in her limbs increased, and Elizabeth silently cursed herself for it. She should not fear this man; he had already done his worst to her.

Not wishing to dwell on the viscount's face, Elizabeth turned her gaze to her mother, who watched her with a stern expression. No doubt she planned to reiterate her insistence that Elizabeth accept the man's proposal. Jane was the only one regarding Elizabeth with any sympathy. Elizabeth did not acknowledge Lord Henry's presence. "I have a headache, Mama, and must retire to my room."

Her mother drew herself up to her full height. "Lizzy! Lord Henry has come all this way to see you! He wishes to speak with you *in particular*. It is quite an honor."

Elizabeth shook her head vigorously. "No, Mama. I am a good deal too ill…"

Mrs. Bennet stood. "I am certain what he has to say will not take too long." Her expression was severe and implacable. She walked toward the doorway, brushing past Elizabeth and whispering in her ear. "This foolishness has gone on long enough. You must accept this man for the sake of your family. Only you can undo the damage you have caused."

Elizabeth kept her face blank despite the plunging despair that gripped her heart. Lord Henry's smile grew more predatory; no doubt he guessed the instructions her mother had hissed at her.

Jane's face was stricken; she had not moved from her chair. "Come, Jane," their mother said sharply.

Jane cleared her throat. "Mama, I thought I might keep Lizzy company." Elizabeth silently gave thanks for her sister.

"Nonsense!" Mrs. Bennet exclaimed. "Lord Henry must speak with Lizzy privately." Jane hesitated. "Come along!" she hissed impatiently.

Elizabeth nodded permission to Jane. She planned to pass a mere minute in Lord Henry's presence—just long enough to demand that he leave—before she quitted the room.

Jane stood reluctantly and exited, closing the door softly behind her.

Instantly, the viscount was out of his seat, stalking toward Elizabeth. Heart pounding, she pressed herself against the door, grasping the knob in her hand in case she needed to make a hasty retreat. Who would have guessed he would display such predatory behavior in her own home?

He stopped a mere foot from her. "You think you are so clever," he hissed. "Denying me for so long! Do you think that you can hold out for a better marriage settlement?"

Elizabeth swallowed. "No. I have no intention of ever accepting your offer."

She plastered herself against the door as if she could somehow escape through solid wood. He stood quite a bit closer than propriety allowed but made no move to touch her. "Darcy will not rescue you," he sneered. "He left Hertfordshire without you. You are too soiled even for his liking."

Elizabeth clenched her teeth against any objections. It would do her no good if Lord Henry knew the truth, and it might hurt Mr. Darcy.

He leaned so close that she could smell his sour breath. "If you do not accept my offer of marriage, you eventually will be forced to depend on me on less…favorable terms. Do you understand?" There it was, the threat of making her his mistress—just as Mr. Darcy had warned her. "You should accept my offer…while it is still available."

Elizabeth squeezed the doorknob more tightly and reminded herself of Mr. Darcy's words about Lord Henry. So far he had behaved just as Mr. Darcy had predicted. She lifted her chin, although the trembling in her limbs no doubt belied any show of defiance. "Is there anything else, sir? I would like to go upstairs for a rest."

Lord Henry uttered an inarticulate growl. Then he pressed the entire length of his body against hers. His thighs pushed against hers. His stomach rubbed hers. His arms pressed into the door on either side of her head, caging her in. However, as his face neared hers, she turned her head to the side so that the kiss landed on her cheek. "Bah!" he exclaimed. "No

woman has ever given me so much trouble. But it will come to an end."
He gave a harsh laugh.

"Sir, my father is in the house. He will not be pleased that you—"

He stepped away from her, holding his hands in the air. "Very well. I will go." He pointed a finger in her face. "But I have been very patient so far, *Lizzy*. My patience is nearing the end. The next time I see you, you will be mine…one way or another."

Elizabeth barely had time to move out of the way before the viscount flung open the door and stomped out of the house.

She leaned against the drawing room wall, now allowing the tears to fall and her limbs to shake. The tap of heels and swish of skirts announced the return of her mother and Jane. "Oh, Lizzy!" Jane cried. Elizabeth fell gratefully into her sister's warm embrace.

"So you spurned him again, did you?" Her mother's voice was shrill. "I must speak with your father about this stubbornness, Lizzy. We cannot condone it forever."

Elizabeth kept her eyes screwed tightly shut to avoid her mother's disapproving expression. She knew her father would not expect her to marry the viscount, but Lord Henry's threats caused her heart to ache for a different reason.

He had made it clear that he would not forget her, nor would he accept her refusal. And her presence at Longbourn brought his wrath upon her and her family. It could not continue. She had to go away. She could no longer call Longbourn her home.

***

"I wish you would reconsider, Lizzy," her father said for at least the third time, fiddling nervously with the letter opener on his desk. "At least wait until the Gardiners return to London."

"It could be months," Elizabeth responded. The entire family had gone north for a trip concerning her Uncle Gardiner's business, and the date of their return was not fixed. Secretly Elizabeth was relieved. While staying with Gardiners would have been pleasant, she had no doubt that news of her disgrace had reached London, and she had no desire to inflict her scandal upon them.

"At least you may stay at Gracechurch Street when you arrive. The servants are quite accommodating."

Elizabeth nodded as she stared down at the hands clasped in her lap. There was no need to tell her father she did not have the least intention of spending even a night at the Gardiners' house if she could avoid it. It would be best if no one knew the family was associated with the "wayward" Elizabeth Bennet.

Her father sighed and leaned back in his chair. "All the excitement over the viscount's story will die down in a few months, and then you may return to us." Elizabeth nodded again, but she did not hold much hope that the memory of her disgrace would fade so rapidly.

Opening a draw of his desk, her father pulled out a purse that clinked when he set it on the desk before her. "You will need some cash for the journey." A bit apprehensively, Elizabeth opened the purse and peered inside. "Oh no, Papa! This is too much."

She tried to hand it back to him, but he waved her gesture away. "I only wish I could give you more. But that is all the ready cash I have to hand."

"'Tis too much, Papa. Surely you will have need of it here." She had already cost her family dearly in terms of reputation; she did not want to be financial burden as well.

Mr. Bennet removed his glasses and rubbed his eyes with one hand. "London is expensive, child. You will require more than wits to survive."

"I plan to find a position as a governess," she said hastily.

Her father's head jerked up, startled. He knew she would not seek out such a position if she had any hope of repairing her reputation and marrying a respectable man. She met his gaze. After a moment he sighed as he replaced his glasses. "Take the money, Lizzy. No doubt you will have need of it." He fixed her with a rather stern frown.

Elizabeth's hand closed around the purse. "Very well. Thank you, Papa."

Her father leaned forward, resting his elbows on the desk. "Write to us frequently, Lizzy. I will worry about you every day." He blinked back some suspicious moisture in his eyes.

Elizabeth hastily wiped her own. "Of course. I plan to tell nobody where I am going, save Jane. I do not want word to reach the viscount, and Kitty or Lydia might—"

He gave a dry chuckle. "No need to convince me, my dear. Kitty or Lydia or even your mother are not the souls of discretion. I will tell nobody."

"Thank you for your help, Papa." She stood, wishing she could stay in her father's study forever. But the longer she remained, the harder it would be to leave.

Her father stood as well; he walked around the desk and drew her into an embrace, kissing her forehead. "I would not part with you for all the world," he murmured. "But you have been dealt with very unfairly. Perhaps your fortunes will improve in London."

Elizabeth nodded, not trusting herself to speak. If only she had her father's optimism. She gave him a quick kiss on the cheek and hurried from the room before he noticed her tears.

***

It had been nearly three weeks since he had departed from Hertfordshire. During his more optimistic moments, Darcy hoped to hear from Elizabeth. Before leaving, he had given her directions where to find him either in London or in Derbyshire—and even the name and address of his man of business should she need any funds. Although he knew there was little chance she would accept his money, it eased his heart. She had accepted the information graciously, and every day he prayed she would avail herself of it despite the impropriety of writing to an unmarried man.

At other times he knew he was fooling himself. She would not contact him any more than she would accept his offer of marriage. She might be grateful for his support, but she would not compromise her honor or sacrifice her pride by asking for help. In his darkest moments, he recalled how she bade him goodbye as if she would never again lay eyes upon him, and he wondered if perhaps she had declined the offer because she did not want to be married to him.

Darcy had asked Netherfield's housekeeper—with the incentive of a generous bonus—to contact him should she hear any news of significance about Elizabeth or the family at Longbourn. *I should have asked her to write me weekly even if there is no news. This lack of information is galling.*

Every day he sought distraction, fighting to keep worries about Elizabeth at bay. Was her family being kind to her? Did she need money? Had the viscount made another attempt to compromise her? Were the people of Meryton still treating her like a pariah?

Today Darcy had been trying to bury himself in the estate accounts his steward had sent from Pemberley, but as always, visions of Elizabeth crept into his thoughts. Her smile. The way she tipped her head to the side. Her trilling laughter.

When a footman delivered the day's post to his desk, Darcy was ready for a respite. As always, he immediately browsed through the letters for anything from Elizabeth. His heart stuttered when he saw a letter from Meryton addressed in feminine handwriting, but another glance told him it had been posted from Netherfield. Then it was from Cranston, the housekeeper. Scarcely less eager, he forced himself to open it slowly lest he tear the fragile paper.

Dear Mr. Darcy,

You had instructed me to write to you with any news concerning the Bennet family at Longbourn, particularly relating to Miss Elizabeth Bennet. I have not written until now because there was nothing of note to report. However, yesterday I learned of something which happened some days before but only now came to light. Miss Elizabeth has departed from Longbourn and is no longer in residence there, having quitted the house at least two days ago and possibly longer.

I inquired as unobtrusively as possible about her whereabouts but was singularly unsuccessful in gaining any information. No one in town and none of the staff at Longbourn seem to know where she might have gone, although her absence is much remarked upon. The Bennet family has been entirely silent on the subject, which must be quite a burden for Mrs. Bennet, if you catch my meaning. Their housekeeper, Hill, told me that Mrs. Bennet has relatives in London—the Gardiner family on Gracechurch Street. However, they are not presently in residence. Hill did not know of any other relatives whom Miss Elizabeth might visit.

You did not ask this of me, but I thought you might find it interesting to know that Lord Henry remains in residence with his aunt at Felham Hall. I apologize for not giving you better or more complete information. I will write again should I gain further information about Miss Elizabeth's whereabouts.

Yours, etc.

Mary Cranston

Darcy's heart was pounding by the time he laid the letter on his desk. At least while Elizabeth resided at Longbourn, Darcy had been reassured about her safety. But now he knew neither her whereabouts nor her circumstances. She could be anywhere in England and in dire need of help—and Darcy would not know. He crumpled the letter in frustration.

At least he had hired the right spy. Mrs. Cranston had gone far beyond his initial commission to obtain information for him. She had allayed his first fear: that Lord Henry had somehow spirited Elizabeth away. In that case, the viscount would not have remained in residence at Felham.

It seemed likely that the Bennet family had sent her away. For her protection? Or because of her disgrace?

More importantly, where would they have sent her? He wished he knew more about the family's lineage and background. But most of his residency in Hertfordshire had been consumed with the desire to avoid their company. The only relative he knew was Mr. Collins, hardly the person she would ask for help.

If the Gardiners were at home, she might have gone to them, but at the moment the information was worthless. Undoubtedly the Bennet family had other relatives in remote corners of England, but how could Darcy learn their identities?

If only she had turned to him instead of disappearing! Darcy would have moved heaven and earth to ensure Elizabeth's safety, even if she would never be his wife.

Closing his eyes, Darcy rubbed his forehead with one hand. His first impulse was to ride to Longbourn and demand—well, beg—her family to reveal her whereabouts. However, it would be an exercise in mortification, and it was unlikely to be successful. It was unlikely Elizabeth had revealed his proposal, so his sudden interest in her would be rather shocking to the family, if not suspicious. He would also face Mrs. Bennet's attempts to foist a different daughter on him, a thought that rendered him slightly nauseous.

He thrust his hands into his short curls and tugged as though the pain could help him concentrate. Damnation! There had to be some way to find her.

He reviewed all the options once more but arrived at the same conclusion.

His breathing grew more rapid. What if he never found her? What if she were forever lost to him? It did not bear thinking about.

Darcy crumpled the letter into a ball and threw it savagely to the floor.

***

"No, I'm sorry. We don't have any positions." The woman was younger than Elizabeth, and her face reflected genuine regret, which was an improvement over the last place. There the shop owner had said "begone with you now" and made shooing motions when Elizabeth revealed her lack of prior experience.

"Do you know anywhere that might be hiring? Anywhere in London?" Elizabeth asked the regretful young woman.

The other woman shook her head. "Not many places are. Times are hard."

Elizabeth nodded; she had learned that herself. As she navigated her way out of the milliner's shop, she considered her situation. *I always thought of myself as well-educated and moderately skillful, until I started looking for a position.*

There was no money in being adequate at playing the pianoforte or fairly good at embroidery. Her scattershot education in history and bits of mathematics and French would do her no good either. And she knew nothing about the workings of her kitchen; her mother had been particularly proud of that. Now she saw that she had only ever been trained to be someone's wife. When that position was no longer available, she had nothing to offer in exchange for gainful employment. It was a rather lowering experience.

Elizabeth had visited milliners' and haberdashers' establishments on the strength of her sewing, but they all wanted someone with prior experience. Truthfully, she was not certain her stitching would be good enough to hold a position if she obtained one.

I might have made a good governess. But the first agency she approached wanted a character reference from someone who was not a member of her family. Elizabeth immediately realized that any inquiry about her in Meryton would reveal the scandal. Nobody would hire her to supervise their children.

Each morning she perused the papers for a suitable position but had found few opportunities. So she trod the streets every day, applying at shops with "help needed" signs in the window—and some that did not.

She wrapped her shawl more tightly around her shoulders. The early March weather had turned bitterly cold, and her pelisse was not warm enough by itself. Daily trudging along the pavements of London was wearing down the soles of her half boots, and she could feel the coldness of the slate under her feet. *How long do I have until one of them has a hole?* She was not certain she could afford a repair.

London was expensive, and week by week her expenses for lodging and food ate away at her small nest egg. If she did not find gainful employment soon…Elizabeth shuddered. Best not to think of that. Every day it grew a little more difficult to keep a positive attitude.

There was still a scrap of sunlight in the afternoon sky, but Elizabeth decided to call it a day, plodding toward her lodging house. There were only so many times she could face rejection in one day. She barely had the energy to reach Cheapside as it was.

To distract herself from the aches in her feet, she thought about Mr. Darcy. She knew she would never see him again, yet somehow imagining his dark curls and solemn smile or the sound of his deep baritone cheered her at such moments. She had done the right thing by refusing his proposal. She did not regret it.

She did not.

But when things were very bleak, she allowed herself the fantasy that he did love her. She knew it was a foolish dream. Even if she had been free to accept his proposal, his insulting words about her family most likely would have prevented it. But sometimes she needed the fantasy— to imagine a loving husband, a warm home, perhaps children someday. All of those things which she would never have…

The lodging house was not far from the Gardiners' home. Elizabeth had refused the housekeeper's offer to stay at the Gracechurch Street house, but had been grateful when Mrs. Greene gave her the name of a woman letting rooms in her house to "women of good character." Mrs. Greene had vouched for Elizabeth's character to the landlady, Mrs. Haskell. Without that endorsement, Elizabeth would not have acquired the luxury of a narrow room with a hard bed and two hooks on which to hang her clothing.

Mrs. Haskell had a strict sense of right and wrong, and Elizabeth strove to stay on her good side. She paid her rent punctually every week and engaged her landlady in pleasant conversation whenever possible. Still, the woman's attitude had not noticeably warmed.

Elizabeth sighed with relief when she reached the boarding house and stumbled gratefully up the short walk to the door. Elizabeth fitted the key into the lock, and the front door swung open. Lovely warmth enveloped her as she entered the house, but somehow today it was not quite warm enough. She shivered violently. It must have been colder than she thought outdoors.

"Good day, M-Mrs. Haskell," she greeted her landlady. The woman sat in the drawing room, knitting needles clicking as she created something she swore would be mittens. But Elizabeth could not discern a mitten shape in the mess of stitches and thought the woman would be lucky if the project yielded a usable muffler.

"Miss Bennet. I found a glove on the floor in your room," the older woman replied without slowing the speed of her knitting.

Oh, merciful heavens! The landlady was obsessive about keeping their rooms neat, but seriously…a single glove? Elizabeth did her best to look contrite. "I will strive to do better in the future."

Mrs. Haskell sniffed, her eyes still on her knitting. "See that you do."

Following that cheerful greeting, Elizabeth began her ascent of the narrow stairs to her second-floor room. By the time she reached the top step, she was panting—and still shivering despite the warmth. How odd. Usually she could climb the stairs briskly with no trouble. She shuffled the few feet to her room, closing the door behind her. It was time to change for dinner, but the bed beckoned, reminding her how lovely it would be to lie down. Just for a minute.

Without warning, Elizabeth began to cough, rattling her lungs and her head. She sank onto the bed until the fit passed. Thoughts ground sluggishly through her mind. The cough reminded her of something. Another person with a cough. Oh. Anne from upstairs had had a similar-sounding cough. She had been sick for weeks. The other boarders had been subject to a constant stream of Mrs. Haskell's complaints about the illness and doctors' visits at all times of the day.

But I cannot fall ill. I must go out tomorrow and seek another job. Today she had identified a street that she had not previously investigated.

Still, the pillow called to her enticingly. Her arms and legs would ache less if she lay down for a bit. *I can rest a little and then change my clothing.* She dropped her head onto the pillow and lifted her feet to the end of the bed, unconcerned even about her boots on the counterpane. *I will rest for a short time. Just a few minutes…*

Chapter Nine

Darcy had been unable to banish Elizabeth Bennet from his mind. It had been weeks since receiving the troubling missive from the Netherfield housekeeper, and he was no closer to discovering her location. His investigator had confirmed that the Gardiners' Gracechurch Street home was inhabited only by servants. Venturing to Meryton, the man made discreet inquiries about the Bennet family's relations but had discovered nobody who might be hosting a wayward relative.

At first Darcy tried to convince himself that he could survive without the knowledge. After all, she was not a relative or his betrothed; her whereabouts were not his business. And surely Mr. and Mrs. Bennet would have sent their daughter somewhere safe. Then he thought about Mrs. Bennet shrieking and fluttering her hands, or Mr. Bennet idly reading in his study while the household fell into chaos around him. Then he was inclined to panic.

He reminded himself that she had declined his proposal and all offers of help; he was not responsible for her wellbeing. But his heart did not understand this reasoning. It simply wanted Elizabeth, whole and unharmed, preferably in Darcy House. Every moment of every day was shadowed by the knowledge that the woman he loved was somewhere in England—perhaps lost or in danger.

Darcy had finally decided he must travel to Longbourn himself. He hoped to persuade Elizabeth's father to reveal her location, although it would not be easy. Most likely Mr. Bennet would assume Darcy's interest was inappropriate. But if that plan failed, Darcy hoped he might convince one of Elizabeth's careless younger sisters to let something slip. Once he made the decision, Darcy's spirits felt lighter. It would be good to take some kind of action.

As luck would have it, that day's post prompted a change in plans.

He was eating breakfast with Georgiana when a footman placed the morning post on the table. Perusing the pile of letters, Darcy found one from Hertfordshire in a feminine script—most definitely not Mrs. Cranston's bold hand. Was it possible Elizabeth had returned home and was now writing to him for help? What a relief it would be!

"Excuse me, dearest," he said to his sister, who was describing a new piece of music she was learning. "This is a matter of some urgency."

"Of course." Georgiana eyed the letter with concern.

He tore the letter open with trembling hands. His eyes immediately darted to the signature at the bottom: "Yours, etc. Jane Bennet."

Jane Bennet!

Why would Miss Bennet write to him? It was the height of impropriety. Darcy's anxiety instantly multiplied. Circumstances must be dire.

He read the letter hastily.

Dear Sir,

I pray you, forgive me for being so forward as to write you in this manner. It is only desperation that drives me to such lengths, and I rely on your discretion to conceal my impropriety. The matter is of some urgency. It concerns my sister Elizabeth. She had related to me that you had expressed some concern for her welfare and had given her a paper with your direction on it (which remains here at Longbourn). I believe she may be in need, and you may be in a position to help her.

Elizabeth left Longbourn approximately three weeks ago after an encounter with Lord Henry convinced her that he would continue to press his suit in a most distressing manner. Desiring to stem gossip, she confided her destination only to me and our father.

Her intention was to find a room to let in London and seek employment there. Although my father and I had some misgivings about her safety, she was determined to follow the plan. We received letters from her after her arrival in London. She had found lodging with a friend of the Gardiners' housekeeper but did not give us the address. Her landlady did not want her receiving letters at the house, so we continued to send them to the Gardiners' house on Gracechurch Street, where she collected them every few days.

Her letters stopped suddenly a few days ago. We wrote to the Gardiners' housekeeper to ask if she had seen Elizabeth but have not received word from her either. I do not know what to think. An attack of gout has prevented my father from journeying to London to seek her. My sister has always been a faithful correspondent with me, and I fear for her wellbeing.

Perhaps I presume too much upon friendship to ask you to investigate the matter, and if so, please burn this letter and forget my inquiry. But I beg you for the sake of any affection you still bear for her, please look for my sister. I fear you may be the only person who can locate her.

Thank you and God bless you.

Yours, etc.
Jane Bennet

When he finished the letter, Darcy fell against the back of the chair with a thump. Elizabeth missing? Her whereabouts a mystery even to her own family? His mind conjured visions of all the terrible fates that could have befallen her. The missive's only piece of good news was that Elizabeth probably remained in London, so he could begin a search immediately. He shifted restlessly in his chair, his whole body eager to start at once.

"William?" Georgiana regarded him with wide eyes. He could only imagine the dark expressions that had crossed his face as he read the letter.

He sighed. It was time to tell the story to his sister. "I have received disturbing information. It concerns the young lady I mentioned before, Elizabeth Bennet. You remember how Miss Bingley related the story of a scandal?" Georgiana nodded. Darcy then proceeded to relate the whole tale, omitting only his feelings about Elizabeth and the proposal.

When he finished, Georgiana's hand was over her mouth, and tears welled in her eyes. "The poor girl!" she exclaimed. "I could have suffered a similar fate if you had not stopped Mr. Wickham. You must do all you can to find her, William!"

"I shall. Believe me." Darcy stood, pushing his chair away from the table. And he knew exactly where to start: Gracechurch Street.

***

Darcy approached the modest brick house with neat curtains and broken shutters. It had been easy to determine why the Gardiners' housekeeper had not responded to the Bennets' inquiries: the woman was in Surrey caring for an ailing mother. Darcy had been required to interview nearly every servant in the Gardiners' household before the cook recalled that Mrs. Greene had a friend who took boarders on Lime Street. As Darcy traversed the cracked pathway up to the front door, he prayed that he would find Elizabeth here. If not, he would not know where else to search.

His knock on the door was answered by a surly-faced frowsy woman with wisps of hair escaping from her white cap. Her expression went from irritated to mildly piqued as she took in Darcy's obvious wealth. "What can I do for you, sir?" she asked. The odor of cooked cabbage wafted from the kitchen.

"I am looking for Elizabeth Bennet. Is she lodging with you?"

Her eyes narrowed. "The girls can't have male visitors."

Darcy ground his back teeth. He had not come so far to be stymied by a stupid rule. "Can you at least tell me if she resides here?"

Her lips pressed together as if she were trying to find a good reason to deny his inquiry. "Yes, she does," the woman said finally.

Relief flooded Darcy's veins. "Is she at home? May I speak with her?"

"Yes, she's here, but she can't take no male visitors."

Oh, for the love of—! "Then will you tell her that I am here and ask her to come outside so we may converse in the street?"

The woman blinked slowly. "I could tell her that. But it wouldn't do much good."

Darcy bit back an angry retort. Why did this woman have to dole out information as if each word cost her money? "Why not?" he asked.

She shrugged. "She's much too ill to come downstairs."

Why was it suddenly so hard to breathe? Politeness be damned; he pushed his way past the woman into her small front hall. "Have you summoned a physician?"

She sneered at him. "I ain't made of money, you know. I did have the apothecary to visit, but he couldn't do nothing. She hasn't even paid me for that, and she owes this week's rent!"

Blast and damnation. This was worse than his worst imaginings. "Is she out of funds?"

"I don't know." The woman shook her head. "She hasn't been awake long enough to ask." Darcy gritted his teeth at the idea that Elizabeth's lucid periods had been full of inquiries about the rent money. "If she dies, I'm having her body taken over to the Gardiners' house, I am. I ain't paying for a funeral."

"Your Christian charity knows no bounds," Darcy said dryly.

The woman stared at him, failing to comprehend his sarcasm.

His patience was officially at an end. "How much does she owe?" he growled at the landlady.

The woman hesitated, obviously wondering how much she could get from him.

"Here." He thrust a guinea into her hand. "Take me to her."

She sniffed. "But I run a respectable house. I cannot allow a man upstairs—"

"What do you possibly think I would do to sick lady, you miserable woman?" Two strides took him to the bottom of the stairs, causing the landlady to rush after him. "If you take me to her, I will remove her from this house, and she will cease to be your problem. If you do not take me to her immediately, I will proceed upstairs and open every door in this place until I find her."

His words lit a fire under the woman. She hastened up the stairs with Darcy hard on her heels.

At the top of the stairs, she turned right and opened a narrow door. He followed her into a tiny room, dim even in the late morning light. The landlady marched to the window and drew back the curtains. Weak sunshine flooded the room, revealing that indeed Elizabeth was lying on the bed.

But she bore little resemblance to the woman he had last seen in Hertfordshire. She was quite a bit thinner, and her skin was pale, almost translucent in places. Dark purple smudges shadowed each eye. Cracked lips suggested that it had been a while since she had been given any water. A quick touch to her forehead confirmed that she was burning up with fever. She lay completely still, her only movement the labored up and down of her chest.

Darcy's heart pounded a fast drumbeat and breathing became difficult. He fought the sense of dread welling up inside of him. *I cannot panic; I am Elizabeth's only hope.*

Good God in Heaven, Darcy prayed desperately. *Let me not be too late!*

She needed to leave this place, and she needed a doctor. There was no time to waste. Deciding to take her to Darcy House, he wrapped the blankets around Elizabeth's thin frame, alarmed that his actions did not rouse her in the slightest. The March day was mild, but he did not want to take the chance she might be chilled.

"Oi! Those be my blankets!" the landlady exclaimed.

Darcy glared at her. "You have been more than adequately compensated. Now pack up her things so I may take them as well."

"I ain't your servant!" The woman folded her arms over her chest indignantly.

"If you do not, I will send my footman to do it, and that will not do the reputation of your house any good," he growled.

Grumbling, the woman set to work gathering Elizabeth's clothing, which she packed rather haphazardly in the small trunk at the foot of the bed.

Darcy picked up Elizabeth, disturbed at how little effort it took, and carried her down the narrow stairs and out of the front door. The landlady followed with the trunk. He strode quickly to his carriage, wishing to minimize Elizabeth's exposure to the wind and cold. Grimm, his driver, stared for a moment at the sight of his master carrying an unconscious woman but then hastened to open the carriage door. Darcy laid her carefully on the seat. She had not roused throughout the entire ordeal.

"Grimm," Darcy called to the groom. "Please fetch Miss Bennet's trunk."

The man glanced back at the landlady standing sullenly in the doorway, nodded, and closed the carriage door. A few bumps and jostles told Darcy that Grimm had secured the trunk on the back of the carriage, and soon it lurched into motion.

Sitting beside Elizabeth, Darcy stroked her hair gently. "That is the last you will see of that wretched place, my love," he promised her. "But I need you to hold on—for my sake. I cannot lose you now."

***

Georgiana's eyes nearly bulged out of her head when her brother carried an unconscious woman through the front door of Darcy House. Once he explained the circumstances, however, she sprang into action, sending a footman for the family doctor and having the maids lay a fire in the rose bedchamber. Darcy set Elizabeth gently on the bed, almost regretting that he could not continue to keep her in his arms; holding her felt completely right and natural.

Georgiana then shooed him out of the room while Mrs. Greenwood, the housekeeper, and Phillips, the upstairs maid, changed Elizabeth into a clean gown, settled her under the covers, and bathed her in cool water to bring down the fever.

Darcy had a pile of papers in the study that required his attention, but he could not bear to leave the vicinity of Elizabeth's room. He paced the hallway outside her door, waiting for his sister to emerge. When she did, he peppered her with questions about Elizabeth's condition.

"I do not know." Georgiana shook her head. "I think her color may have improved, but Greenwood had no luck getting her to drink. Hopefully the doctor will arrive quickly."

Darcy was not good at waiting under the best of circumstances, but with the fate of the woman he loved in the balance…the delay had the potential to drive him mad. Despite the impropriety, he wanted to be in her room. He knew the sight of her sunken cheeks and pallor would twist his stomach into knots, yet he *needed* to see her and reassure himself that she still breathed. Being separated from her made her life feel all the more fragile to him.

He had been prepared for the idea that she might never be his wife, but not for this —never for this. How could he live in a world that did not somewhere contain Elizabeth Bennet? He pressed his fist against his mouth to muffle a moan.

After what seemed an eternity, Dr. Hanson arrived. His cravat was askew and his hair was unkempt, as if the Darcy House footman had dragged him from his home before he had a chance to glance in the mirror.

Darcy approved.

Propriety be damned, Darcy followed the physician into Elizabeth's room and observed his examination. But the doctor's every murmur or exclamation of "hmm," caused Darcy's pulse to race. Soon he retreated to the hallway, where Georgiana joined his anxious vigil.

Finally, the doctor slipped out of the chamber, closing the door softly behind him. Georgiana and Darcy both regarded Hanson with worried eyes. His expression was grim. "Miss Bennet has a fever and an infection in her lungs. My guess is that it has been untreated for several days and thus has reached an advanced state."

Darcy wanted to return to Lime Street and strangle the landlady.

"She is young and strong, but the illness has taken a powerful hold." The doctor folded his arms over his chest. "Frankly, I would have expected her to be on the mend by this stage of the illness. I do not like that she is still so sick." The man sighed. "We can only wait and pray for her return to health. But you must prepare yourself for the worst."

Darcy felt as if he had fallen through the ice into freezing water, and now he was gasping for breath. Surely…surely it could not be so dire. He could not have found her again only to lose her in such a way. Fate could not be so cruel. "There must be something you can do for her. Some medicine," he said to the doctor, but the man only shook his head.

The world tilted, and Darcy reached out blindly for the wall to steady himself. Hanson cried, "Here now!" and grabbed his other arm.

The doctor held him while Georgiana pulled a chair out of the bedchamber across the hall and glared at Darcy until he sat in it. "Do not rush to stand up," Hanson warned. "I do not need another patient in this house." He grinned at his little joke, but Darcy could not bring himself to return it. Instead, he leaned forward, cradling his head in his hands.

"What can we do for her?" Georgiana asked the physician.

"Bathe her in cool water as you have been doing to keep down the fever. Make sure she drinks water. Fevers can dehydrate a body."

Darcy should stand, shake the doctor's hand, thank him for coming, and walk the man to the entrance, but he could not move. A leaden weariness had crept into his muscles, and his limbs were suddenly too heavy to move even the smallest inch.

He watched Georgiana thank the man and escort him down the front staircase. *Elizabeth might die. I can do nothing.* The thoughts circled around and around obsessively, not permitting any other thoughts in.

After a minute, he realized Georgiana was standing before him. They exchanged grim looks. "I will have Mrs. Greenwood and Phillips take turns sitting with Miss Bennet during the night," Georgiana said.

"No." Darcy was on his feet without having decided to stand. "I will sit with her." Fortunately, his legs stayed firmly beneath him.

Georgiana frowned at him. "You cannot. She is young, unmarried, and—"

"She is hardly in a state where I could take advantage of her, and I cannot—" His voice cracked. He swallowed and spoke again. "I cannot be apart from her. Not now."

Georgiana tipped her head to the side as she considered. "I suppose her reputation is compromised already…"

"Through no fault of her own," Darcy said sharply.

She sighed. "I did not intend to imply otherwise." Pursing her lips, Georgiana lingered at the door to Elizabeth's room. "Phillips and I can take turns sitting with you. If she awakes feverish and disoriented, she might be scared to be alone with a man."

Darcy could envision such a scenario all too clearly. He had not been considering things from Elizabeth's perspective. Bless Georgiana for thinking of such things! "When did you grow so wise?" he asked.

Georgiana gave him an impish grin. "We should be thankful, Brother, that Mrs. Annesley has gone to visit her son in Newcastle." Darcy could imagine what the very proper lady's companion would have to say. "She would not have approved of this arrangement."

Darcy breathed out a laugh. "Indeed not."

***

The sick room was deathly quiet aside from the grating sounds of labored breathing from Elizabeth's bed and the occasional rustling of bed covers. The doctor had recommended a roaring fire, so it was stiflingly warm with the cloying smell that all sick rooms seemed to acquire. Darcy stripped down to his shirtsleeves and removed his cravat. He was seized by a need to pace, but he dared not move from Elizabeth's side.

Three times she had taken a lengthy pause before another gasping breath. Each time, Darcy had frantically surged to his feet, fearing the worst, only to fall back into his chair with relief when she resumed normal breathing. He dreaded hearing another such pause, and anxiety prevented him from leaving her side for a second, although deep in his heart he knew there was nothing *he* could do to ensure she continued to breathe.

He did what he could to ensure her comfort. At first Phillips bathed Elizabeth's forehead and neck in water to cool the fever, but Darcy soon insisted on taking over the task, prompting raised eyebrows from the maid. He could not articulate to her why he had to do it, only that he did not want to waste any opportunity to care for her.

The situation had eerie echoes of the long vigil by his father's bedside during his final illness, a parallel Darcy did not find reassuring. He prayed, begging and pleading with God with a fervor he had never before experienced. He would do anything—be anything—that Elizabeth required as long as she survived. Even if she were determined never to see Darcy again... The pain of that thought made him catch his breath. But even banishment from her presence would be far better than losing her forever.

If only he could have the briefest glimpse of her sparkling blue eyes! But they remained firmly closed. The figure in the bed scarcely seemed like Elizabeth without her fine eyes, alive with wit and merriment. Her smile was absent as well. He was accustomed to seeing those slack lips animated with humor and ready with a quip. Such simple things, easily taken for granted. At the moment nothing in the world would make him happier than to see her smile and her eyes.

If God granted him another opportunity, he vowed, he would not allow her to slip away from him again.

After several hours the silence grated on him, so Darcy sent Phillips to fetch a few volumes of Shakespeare from the library. He read aloud several of his favorite sonnets to Elizabeth. Then he started on *King Lear*, which Elizabeth had once declared a favorite. However, the darkness of the play weighed down his spirits, and Darcy switched instead to *As You Like It*, a work he could easily imagine Elizabeth enjoying.

Around midnight, Elizabeth's health took a turn, but not for the better. At first she moved restlessly, mumbling incoherent nothings into the pillows. Then her movements became more agitated. In the grips of a high fever, she thrashed about, pulling out the bed covers, breathing rapidly, and crying out wordlessly. One flailing arm actually dealt a glancing blow to Darcy's cheek.

Alarmed, Darcy sent again for Dr. Hanson, who labeled the agitation the result of febrile phantasms and claimed there was nothing to be done. "The fever will break during the night...or it will not," Hanson proclaimed.

After Hanson's departure, Georgiana took Phillips's place. Brother and sister developed a routine of applying wet cloths and attempting, with some success, to get Elizabeth to sip a bit of water. Darcy clung to Elizabeth's hand, stroking her arm and kissing her fingertips, hoping to soothe her. Soon the thrashing stopped, and Elizabeth rested quietly, but the fever showed no signs of improvement.

At about two in the morning, Georgiana could no longer keep her eyes open, and Darcy sent her to her bedchamber over her objections.

Despite Darcy's fatigue, restless energy coursed through his body until he could no longer bear to sit by Elizabeth's bedside. He paced endlessly around the room, attempting to banish visions of the worst that could happen. After long minutes of prowling around the furniture, it seemed the most natural thing in the world to speak with Elizabeth—even in her unconscious state.

"You cannot die, Elizabeth," he growled at her. "You cannot! I have only just found you again after weeks of uncertainty and days of frantic searching. I cannot lose you now. Do not leave me and force me to live in a world where you do not exist!" Darcy realized he was shouting as he loomed over Elizabeth's bed. He fell back into a chair and dropped his head into his hands.

There was no sense in berating a sick woman. The situation was not of her choosing. Yet Darcy could not seem to calm the anger seething in his veins

The anxiety drove him to pace again; perhaps it gave the illusion that somehow he could outrun his fate.

After several minutes of pacing, Darcy stopped in the middle of the room, regarding Elizabeth with beseeching eyes. "We have never even kissed! Although I imagined it many times. How your lips would feel…how your mouth would taste…how your hair would feel in my fingers…and yet we have not kissed." His voice cracked, and he paused for a moment. "If you leave me, you rob me of the opportunity to experience these things…if you would allow them."

Her face was gaunt and flushed, yet it was still the most beautiful face he had ever beheld. "I have permitted myself the fantasy that you would allow my kisses…or, dare I think, welcome them." He gave a wry chuckle. "If you think otherwise, you must wake and berate me for it." His fingers squeezed the footboard until they turned white. "I would even welcome that. Of course, I would try to change your mind…" At this point a lump in his throat prevented further speech. Darcy let his head drop as he struggled to regain his composure.

He strode back to her bedside and took a limp hand in his, stroking it gently. "I had planned to spend days discovering your preferences. Do you like to have your hair brushed? Is your neck sensitive to kisses? How would you like it if I stroked your cheek thus?" His finger brushed softly down one cheek. "Does that give you pleasure?" His eyes burned, and he swallowed hard.

"I pray you, do not leave me! I could make you so happy if you stay." He inched his chair closer to the bed. "There are so many things I want to share with you. You have never met Georgiana or seen Pemberley—and they are the poorer for it. They need you, too, even if they do not know it." He kissed the palm of her hand, the soft skin on the inside of her wrist.

Tears rolled down his cheeks unchecked.

Finally, he stood, folding her hand over her breast with the other one. In this pose, she resembled the carved stone effigies that marked tombs in Westminster Abbey, a comparison he desperately wanted to forget. "Do not leave me," he pleaded softly. "I want that first kiss…" Then he bowed his head and prayed fervently.

Elizabeth no longer thrashed, but now her head turned, and her hands moved restlessly over the covers. Darcy stroked Elizabeth's long dark curls, running his fingers from the crown of her head to her shoulders. The movement soothed some of her agitation.

Darcy knew he should sleep, and yet he could not tear his eyes from her. He could not bear to lose one moment by her side.

Later, as he brushed his fingers down the side of her cheek, her head turned, and she nuzzled her face into his palm like a wild animal that had decided to trust him. Darcy's breath caught, and he froze in place. She sighed—a sweet, contented sound—and fell into a deep, very still sleep.

Darcy did not dare move his hand. Resting her face against his palm seemed to bring her such pleasure that he would have gladly left it there for all eternity. Eventually, she turned her head in the other direction, allowing Darcy to extricate his hand, but Napoleon's troops could not have dragged him from her bedside.

After several hours, Darcy's eyes threatened to close. He crossed his arms on the edge of the bed and pillowed his head on them. Perhaps he could rest just a little.

Chapter Ten

A finger of light from the rising sun stole across Darcy's face, waking him. He jerked upright, appalled that he had drowsed for so long. What if something had happened to Elizabeth?

Standing to examine the patient, he was relieved to see that her color was better; a slight pinkish hue was beginning to replace the terrible gray pallor. Touching the pillow beside her head, he noticed it was drenched in sweat, as were the covers under her chin. The fever must have broken!

Indeed, when he touched her forehead, it was cool under his fingertips. He said a brief prayer of thanks. She might not be completely healed, but now he believed she would recover. "Perhaps we will have that kiss after all," he murmured to her with a grin.

The door opened just a crack, and Georgiana's head poked into the room, her forehead creased with worry. "The fever has broken," he told her in a low voice. "I believe she is much improved."

"Oh, William!" Her exclamation reminded Darcy that this was indeed an occasion for joy. She hurried around the bed to throw herself into Darcy's arms, giving him a hard embrace. Darcy actually laughed, whether at her exuberance or his relief, he could not say.

He clutched Georgiana to his chest, burying his face in her shoulder. "She will be well. She will be well." His eyes burned, and he allowed a few tears to fall onto the shoulder of his sister's muslin nightrail. When she finally released him, tears shone in Georgiana's eyes as well.

***

Elizabeth had been drifting in and out of awareness for a while, never quite awake enough to open her eyes. Her world had been a confused jumble of people talking to her, voices saying incomprehensible words to each other, people moving about the room—and a talking stork visiting Longbourn, but Elizabeth thought that part might have been a dream.

She could not discern anything the people had said and was unsure if it mattered. For a long time, breathing had been a chore, as though a pile of bricks rested on her chest. Her thoughts had been consumed with the effort of drawing air. Now her breathing was delightfully unencumbered, although occasional coughs wracked her body. She no longer felt that cold had burrowed down into the marrow of her bones; in fact, she was warm under the softest covers she ever recalled.

This was not Mrs. Haskell's scratchy wool blanket or lumpy mattress. *Perhaps I should find that somewhat alarming. Where am I?*

Opening her eyes required concerted willpower. Once she had them open, however, her surroundings were, somewhat alarmingly, unfamiliar. Certainly she was not in the house on Lime Street, nor at Longbourn—nor even at the Gardiners' house, where she might conceivably have been taken during an illness.

The bed she inhabited was bigger than any she had ever slept in. It was as soft as a cloud with a great excess of pillows and covers, all in a light pink hue. Golden light streamed through a window framed in pink curtains. The furnishings were ornate —without being ostentatious —solid, and well-made.

Waking up in a strange location made her feel a bit like the heroine of a lurid novel; however, Elizabeth had never read a novel in which the villain had imprisoned the heroine in the lap of luxury.

Elizabeth glanced about to see if anyone else was in the room. Nobody on her right, but she turned her head to the left. A young woman, tall and blonde, was doing embroidery in the chair by her bedside. Elizabeth was reassured. In the novels, kidnappers never embroidered.

The woman's clothing proclaimed that she was not a servant, but she was wholly unfamiliar to Elizabeth. Noticing her gaze, the woman started and jumped up from her chair. "You are awake!" She was almost as surprised to see Elizabeth as Elizabeth was to see her. "How do you feel?"

"Er…" How to answer that question? Tired? Thirsty? Ill? Grateful to be alive? Slightly panicked about where she was? Elizabeth settled on: "Confused." The word emerged as a croak, and Elizabeth coughed to clear her throat.

"Of course!" The woman's eyes darted back and forth as she decided what to do. "I will get…" She did not finish the thought before she strode out of the room, leaving the door ajar. Her voice floated in from the hallway. "William! William! She has awoken!"

William? Do I know a William? Elizabeth attempted to make the sluggish gears in her mind grind more quickly. There was, of course, Sir William Lucas. But he was an unlikely rescuer, and this certainly was not Lucas Lodge. She could not recall any other Williams who might suit.

Boot heels rapping smartly on the hallway floors announced the arrival of a man. The door was pushed open wide. No. It could not be. She must still have a fever that was causing hallucinations.

Mr. Darcy?

Mr. Darcy!

How did he come to be here? For that matter, how did I come to be here?

He did not appear quite as well as the last time she had seen him. His face was pale with dark smudges under his eyes. His hair was disheveled, and his clothing was creased and rumpled. He had no coat on, only a waistcoat over a fine lawn shirt. In fact, Elizabeth noticed with unease that his cravat was missing altogether, leaving the skin of his neck visible where his shirt was undone. Save her father, she had never seen a man in such a state of undress. No doubt she would blush under other circumstances.

His eyes were soft with concern as he gazed upon her. "How are you feeling?"

"B-better," Elizabeth stammered. "But what are you doing here?" Her voice was raspy from disuse.

This elicited the ghost of a grin from the man. "I live here. You are at Darcy House—in Grosvenor Square."

Elizabeth was thoroughly disoriented. It made no sense; she had gone to sleep at the boarding house. She was sure of that. Perhaps she was still dreaming? "How?" she managed to ask.

She had not expected her questions to elicit a dark blush from a man who ordinarily seemed so unflappable. "Yes…er…I…well, that is to say…you were ill…" His voice trailed off.

Elizabeth remembered that much. "And…?"

He stared fixedly at the wall above her head, still blushing. "I-I did not believe your landlady was attending adequately to your needs, so I brought you here."

Oh my, I have caused Mr. Darcy a good deal of trouble.

"How?" she asked.

He swallowed. "I…um…carried you to my carriage, which brought you here." Finally, he met her eyes in something of a challenge. Did he expect her to object to the decisions he had made?

Elizabeth nodded and essayed a small smile.

"I brought in a doctor to attend you," Mr. Darcy continued. "You were…quite ill." The somber expression on his face provoked her guilt. She caused not only trouble but also anguish. *I must leave as soon as I can so I will not be an additional burden.*

Elizabeth struggled into a sitting position, which made her feel more in command, but she was immediately aware that she wore only a thin muslin nightrail. Hastily she pulled the bed covers up almost to her neck. The heat in her face demonstrated that the illness had not carried away her tendency to blush.

Mr. Darcy was blushing as well—and lingering in the open doorway rather than venturing into her room. Elizabeth understood his concern for propriety, but by his own account, the man had carried her into this very room. Her reputation was in tatters as it was. Surely the time for strict propriety was past.

She gestured to the chair next to her bedside. "Please sit."

Mr. Darcy hesitated before striding into the room and taking the seat. However, he left the door conspicuously open. Elizabeth was oddly touched. *He wishes to reassure me that I am safe with him.*

A hundred questions crowded her mind. "How did you find me?" she managed to ask without coughing. "I cannot believe my arrival in London was much discussed among your friends."

His lips twisted in a bitter smile. "It was not easy. I received a letter from your sister—"

"Jane?" Elizabeth asked incredulously.

"Indeed." He grimaced. "Apparently you had not written to Jane for many days. With your relatives away from London, she could think of no one else who might search for you."

Elizabeth pondered this. Jane must have been very concerned to actually write a letter to Mr. Darcy. "How long was I ill?"

"I would estimate nearly a week before I found you."

The time did not seem nearly so long to her, but she remembered very little—only hazy impressions, extreme cold, and excessive coughing.

"You did all this? For me?" It was hard to comprehend.

"I would have done far more if the need had arisen."

She stared at him in perplexity.

He shifted impatiently in his chair. "I told you that I would always be your friend."

He had, but Elizabeth had been uncertain to what extent she could trust that friendship. "I am fortunate indeed to have such friends," she said. "But you did not explain how you found the boarding house."

"Miss Bennet's letter directed me to the Gardiners' house, from which I was referred to your landlady's house." His lips twisted with disgust. "She claims to have summoned the apothecary, but I do not believe you received much care."

"I fear Mrs. Haskell cared more for my purse than for my person," Elizabeth said with a wry smile.

Mr. Darcy frowned. "This is not a matter to be taken lightly. You could have perished!"

Elizabeth imagined Mr. Darcy in that dingy, narrow room looking down at her—ill and insensible to the world—and feared she was blushing again. He must have been quite shocked at the manner in which she was living.

Not able to meet his eyes, she focused on the small flowers embroidered on the coverlet. "Please allow me to apologize for putting you to so much trouble."

"I pray you, do not say so!" Mr. Darcy exploded from the chair with great force. "Do you think I would have preferred to learn of your *death*?"

Elizabeth could only gape at him. She had never seen Mr. Darcy quite so volatile.

He stalked angrily to the door. Elizabeth expected him to leave, but he pivoted sharply and paced carefully back to the chair, grasping the back in his hands. "I wish you had come to me for help," he said.

"You know I could not. It would not have been proper," she retorted with some heat.

He scowled at her. "You *must* accept my assistance now."

She could not suppress a smile. *Master of Pemberley indeed.* "Will you also command me to get well?"

Now he looked a bit chagrined and gave a chuckle. "I would if I could. Still, you must stay, propriety be damned; forgive my language."

His intensity was somewhat amusing. "When the alternative is a life-threatening illness, even the strictest book of etiquette would grant some leeway."

"As if I care what such books say," he grumbled.

Now she laughed. "Do you think to frighten me into better health?"

Instantly, Mr. Darcy was back at her bedside, her hand held gently in his. "I apologize, Elizabeth," he said in a soft voice. Her Christian name on his lips should have sounded wrong, but instead it gave her an unexpected sense of warmth. "I should not speak so…I was simply"—his eyes were unfocused, staring at nothing—" terrified."

Terrified? What could such a man possibly fear?

He clasped her hand in both of his. "When I entered that tiny room and saw you lying on the bed, I feared…I was…not in time." He swallowed hard. "I prayed to God—I begged God—to spare me that fate."

Elizabeth stared at him, not knowing what to think. He had experienced such anguish over a woman who had *declined* his offer of marriage? *He must be violently in love with me.* She had believed she knew the man, but now she doubted she had ever scratched the surface.

He squeezed her hand briefly. "So I pray you, do not apologize for the trouble I took in caring for you."

Elizabeth attempted a more sportive tone. "What *should* I apologize for, pray tell?"

He did not smile at her rejoinder. "For nearly taking yourself from my life." His voice had a raspy edge of desperation. "For not turning to me when you needed help."

Guilt was like an ache in her stomach, but she kept her voice light. "Well, sir, I do apologize. I assure you that causing you distress was not at all my purpose in venturing to London." She glanced about at the immaculate bedchamber and the crisp bed linens. She did not belong here. She would not have belonged here before, but her disgrace only magnified the unseemliness of her presence. "Tomorrow when I am better rested, I shall take the mail coach to Longbourn and trouble you no further."

Mr. Darcy made an inarticulate noise; his face was horrified. "No! You cannot—Dr. Hanson said it will take weeks to fully recover your strength, and the journey—"

"Hertfordshire is not so far," she countered.

His expression was thunderous. "Your family members have not proven themselves to be good caretakers for you, Elizabeth. I will *not* relinquish you into their hands."

Despite being touched by his concern, Elizabeth wanted to make a sharp retort. How dare he criticize her family? But then she considered the last month from his perspective. Perhaps it did appear that her family had been careless. Certainly many inhabitants of Longbourn were too wrapped up in their own concerns to spare much thought for the disgraced daughter. The same could not be said for Mr. Darcy.

"I am exceedingly grateful," Elizabeth said truthfully. "Nobody has ever taken such care of me. Nobody."

Mr. Darcy's eyes widened, and a ghost of a smile played about his lips as if such a statement were the greatest gift she could possibly have given him.

Mr. Darcy spread his arms widely, a gesture that encompassed the whole house. "Then I ask you to please accept my hospitality during your recuperation. Any help I grant you is freely given. You are under no obligation to me, and I will ask for nothing in return." She must have appeared skeptical, for he leaned forward and stared earnestly into her eyes. "You have given your answer to my offer, and I respect it. But please respect the fact that I care for you and want to help you."

Elizabeth was silent for a long time, fiddling with the embroidery on the coverlet. She could not hope to repay Mr. Darcy for the care and expense he had undertaken when she was ill, but if she did not, it was tantamount to accepting a gift from him.

Noting her hesitation, Mr. Darcy said hastily, "At least accept my assistance while you are recovering. Once you are well, we may discuss the future." The strain on his face was quite evident. Elizabeth hated that her illness was taking its toll on him. *And my obstinacy is another blow*, she realized. *That is not fair to him.*

"Y-yes, of course," she said. "I thank you for your care and concern, sir." She gestured to the bedchamber. "If I must be sick, at least I may do so in the lap of luxury."

He nodded, but his brows were still knitted together. "You will remain at Darcy House, then?"

"Yes, until I am sufficiently recovered."

He grinned, an expression Elizabeth did not recall seeing on his face before.

A wave of fatigue abruptly washed over Elizabeth, and she was quite ready to be finished with the conversation. She cleared her throat. "I should rest, but first, who was the woman at my bedside when I awoke?"

A fond smile lit up Mr. Darcy's face. "My sister, Georgiana. May I invite her in so you may be introduced properly?"

Elizabeth returned the smile. "If it is not too much trouble."

"Not at all. Waking up with her at your bedside does not quite constitute a proper introduction."

Elizabeth laughed. "It was a bit…truncated."

Mr. Darcy left and returned with his sister. She was exceedingly shy and soft-spoken, although she appeared to be delighted to meet Elizabeth. She must have known something of Elizabeth's family, but Elizabeth saw no sign of reserve or disapproval. It would be pleasant to become better acquainted with the younger woman.

By the end of the brief conversation, the invalid was quite tired, so Mr. and Miss Darcy left her to rest.

***

As Darcy and Georgiana walked away from Elizabeth's room, his heart sang with joy. *Elizabeth would recover! Elizabeth would be well!*

After a moment, he realized Georgiana was being uncharacteristically silent. He gave her a sidelong glance, raising his eyebrow.

She did not look at him. "When were you planning to tell me that you are in love with Miss Bennet?"

"In love with—?" He stopped in the middle of the hall.

"You cannot possibly deny it." Georgiana turned toward him, folded her arms across her chest, and regarded him skeptically. She had matured considerably in the previous year. He was no longer dealing with an almost-child but a young woman. Only the truth would suffice.

Darcy blew out a breath. "You are right, of course."

"When the letter arrived from her sister, you might have mentioned it." Georgiana's voice was sharp.

"I did not believe it was relevant." He stared at the knots in the floorboards.

Georgiana made a noise that sounded like a laugh. "Relevant?" She took two steps closer, forcing him to look her in the eye. "William, your eyes have never shone so in the presence of a woman. No matter how much disgrace she has experienced, you should ask her to be your wife."

Darcy snorted. "I did."

Georgiana stumbled backward in surprise. "But you said—she rejected you? How could she—?"

Darcy shook his head slowly. "She does not want me and my family to share in her disgrace, and she is not wrong. If I marry a woman mired in scandal, it could materially affect your chances of making a good match."

"I do not care one whit for that!" Georgiana declared stoutly.

He gave a bleak laugh. "You say that now, but you might regret it later."

Georgiana waved that concern away. "I will not suffer, but you...will you ask her again?" Georgiana watched him from the corner of her eye.

"I plan to broach the subject again, yes." He considered. "Perhaps tomorrow when her mind is clearer."

Georgiana laughed.

"What is so amusing, dearest?"

"She is awake for the first time after a weeklong illness, and you will give her *one whole day* to recover before you spring another offer of marriage on her? How magnanimous of you." She chuckled. "For an intelligent man, you are remarkably stupid sometimes."

I cannot possibly wait longer than that, can I? Even now he could barely restrain himself from rushing back to her room and posing the question to her once again. But Georgiana often understood these things better than he did. She was better with people and far better at understanding women than he was. Perhaps she had a point.

"I could wait until she is in better health," he said. Georgiana nodded approvingly. "But it will be torturous. I do not know how long I can hold off."

She gave a small laugh as if she thought he had made a joke, but when she noticed his expression, she immediately sobered.

"Would it make you happy to have a new sister?" Darcy asked.

A small smile played about his sister's lips. "That would make me very happy...as long as she loves you."

"Of course, she loves me," Darcy responded automatically.

One of Georgiana's eyebrows raised. "Did you ask her?"

"Naturally, I—" Darcy shut his mouth with a snap. *I never asked her.* The realization washed over him like a cold bucket of water. *I never inquired about her feelings. I just assumed she loved me. Assumed she would be honored to marry the "great" Fitzwilliam Darcy and—what? Love would come? She would love me out of gratitude? Do I want a wife who feels* grateful *to me? That could not possibly be the foundation for a strong marriage.*

He shoved both hands into his unruly dark curls. "Damnation!" he exclaimed. "Pardon my language, Georgie." He rubbed his forehead. "I...never asked."

Georgiana regarded him sardonically. "You just assumed?" When he said nothing, she sighed. "Do you recall when you declined the Redburns' dinner party invitation without asking me?"

Darcy closed his eyes. They had argued quite extensively over that particular mistake of his. He had assumed she would be as bored at the Redburns' dinner as he would have been, but she had learned that a few of her friends would be there and had been dreadfully disappointed she would not see them. She had refused to speak with Darcy for a week. "I could not possibly forget." He opened his eyes in alarm. "This is not as bad as that, is it?"

Georgiana shook her head, and Darcy relaxed. "It is much worse."

"Oh, damn—" Darcy stopped himself and swallowed convulsively. "Worse? Really?"

She gave one decisive nod. "Yes. Worse. I know you are accustomed to making decisions for others, but you do not always understand another person's mind. You must speak with her about her feelings, William—before you make her another offer. You owe her that courtesy, and you owe it to yourself."

He rubbed his hand over his eyes. It was a failing, he knew, this tendency to try and organize other people's lives. Yet he did not always realize when he was doing it.

"You must ask her about her feelings," his sister repeated firmly. "Ask her if she loves you."

"I will," Darcy promised.

But what will I do if the answer is "no"?

Chapter Eleven

Several days later Darcy knew the moment had arrived. Georgiana had left on a shopping excursion with a friend; it was the ideal opportunity for Darcy to have an uninterrupted conversation with Elizabeth. As he sat in his study, the notes from her practice on the pianoforte floated upstairs from the music room. Darcy could wander into the room, listen to her play, and then strike up a conversation when she finished. They would discuss Mozart and Salieri for a while, and then he could shift the conversation in another direction.

"By the way, are you in love with me?"

Darcy thumped his head down on the desk. That would not work.

Surely there was an easier way. Men had been asking women to marry them for centuries. In all that time, there must have been at least one man who had asked a woman about her feelings for him.

If only Darcy could find that man and ask him for advice.

It should not be that difficult, he told himself. And yet she had already refused him once. He was not eager for another rejection. He could not help wondering if her refusal resulted from dislike rather than fear of scandal. What if he asked her if she loved him—and she demurred?

When he first realized that he had neglected to ascertain Elizabeth's feelings, he had seen it as an oversight. *But perhaps I am better off not knowing.* The prospect of actually raising the subject with her…well, he would have preferred to face Napoleon's troops armed only with a spoon.

In the weeks since he had proposed, Darcy often recalled Elizabeth's words in response. He had expected her to be delighted by his proposal, or at least charmed. While she had been polite, her refusal had not shown signs of great regret. Perhaps that was his answer.

However, in her response she had alluded to his offensive words about her family. Only slowly had he come to realize that such words might have colored her perception of him. Perhaps in his eagerness to tell her of his love, he had not created the best impression upon Elizabeth. He shuddered to think how he would have responded if she had said half of those things about *his* family. *And now I will ask her if she loves me?*

He laughed aloud. *I am a fool.*

Perhaps he should not even bother to approach her, but his heart was a foolish organ and absolutely insisted that Elizabeth was the one he must marry. It refused to give up hope. Even now.

Brandy. That was what he needed.

Darcy stood and poured himself a glass from the crystal decanter on the sideboard. He downed it quickly. He was a fool, yet he had no choice. He must ask her. The brandy spread warmth throughout his body as Darcy considered how to phrase such a question.

"Miss Elizabeth, might you tell me your feelings about me?"

No.

"Miss Elizabeth, I love you. I pray you, tell me if you return the sentiment."

No.

"Elizabeth, for God's sake, tell me what is in your heart!"

Definitely not.

Darcy stood to pour himself another glass. The liquid was harsh going down his throat, but he enjoyed the wonderful tingling warmth that followed.

Perhaps I can do it.

But what will I do if she says she does not love me?

This thought provoked another trip to the sideboard. After a moment's thought, he retrieved the decanter and set it on his desk.

Perhaps speaking to Elizabeth would not be so difficult after all.

***

Over the past few days, Elizabeth's health had gradually improved. Her appetite had increased, and the doctor gave permission for her to venture out of her bed. Her first steps were a bit wobbly, but the strength in her legs returned, and soon she was able to walk around the second floor quite ably—although the effort was initially exhausting. She did not even attempt the stairs until later.

Although Elizabeth hated being a burden, both Darcys seemed delighted at her presence and made her feel quite welcome. Mr. Darcy devoted hours to playing chess with her or reading to her from his favorite books, which often happened to be hers as well. Miss Darcy reveled in having a female companion near to her age. They talked on many subjects, and Elizabeth found Mr. Darcy's sister to be a sweet, engaging companion. When Elizabeth was well enough, she ventured downstairs to the music room to hear Georgiana play the pianoforte, and soon the two women were practicing a duet together.

She had written to Jane with her exact whereabouts but begged her to keep it a secret from the rest of the family. Jane agreed in the next letter, saying that only their father had expressed interest, and Jane had merely assured him that his daughter was safe.

However, there was one way in which Elizabeth's recuperation was less than ideal: she must conceal her presence at Darcy House. Although her reputation was already in tatters, she had no wish to provide anyone with more reasons to label her a loose woman. Nor did she want it known that the Darcys were housing a "fallen woman" under their roof; everyone would make lurid assumptions about Mr. Darcy's relationship with her. Any explanation about illness and recuperation would fall on deaf ears. Just the thought of such gossip brought a blush to Elizabeth's cheeks, and it would be a terrible way to repay the Darcys' generosity.

Mr. Darcy had assured her that his servants could be relied upon to keep his secrets; they were all well-paid and valued their positions. And Dr. Hanson was a family friend who understood the importance of discretion. As the week wore on, it became apparent that word of her visit had not been leaked to the wider world.

Still, Elizabeth lived in fear that the Darcys would receive an unexpected visitor whose gossip would ruin the lives of two people who had been nothing but kind to her. Mr. Darcy had ordered the knocker removed from the front door, an indication that the inhabitants were not receiving visitors, but no doubt its absence generated curiosity. More than once she had volunteered to quit Darcy House, but both Georgiana and Mr. Darcy were quite adamantly against such a plan, particularly while she was still convalescing. Elizabeth was secretly relieved, for she truly had nowhere she could go.

Elizabeth did her best not to chafe at the enforced confinement. At first she was too weak and ill to regret her lack of exercise, but as her health improved, she longed to take walks or at least visit Darcy House's back garden.

Instead, she devoted hours to practicing on the pianoforte, an activity that did not cause too much strain on her body. Elizabeth was finishing up a piece by Mozart when the music room door opened, and Mr. Darcy slipped in. She was surprised to see him. They had frequently been in company together but always with Georgiana or servants in the room. Not since the day she had awakened in the guest bedchamber had Elizabeth been alone with him.

Throughout her stay at Darcy House, Elizabeth had found Mr. Darcy to be something of a conundrum. He cared deeply for her; that much was obvious. He had sought her location in London with great determination, and then he ensured she had the best care possible as she recovered from her illness. Every time she experienced the slightest chill, he offered her a blanket. When she coughed, he asked if she required tea or a visit from the doctor.

But it was difficult to reconcile this solicitous man with the one who had so casually insulted her the first night of their acquaintance or so callously dismissed her family.

Now he stood in the doorway as the last notes of her piece died away. He did not quite seem to be himself. Perhaps his cheeks were a bit flushed? His nose red? And he was swaying slightly. Oh dear, had he caught the illness that had infected her?

"Are you quite well, sir?" she asked.

He gave her a lopsided smile. "Oh, I am fine indeed." He clapped as he strode toward the pianoforte. "That was magnifilicent. Magnilicent." He shook his head and said rather loudly, "Magnificent."

The oddness continues. Elizabeth closed her book of music. "Thank you."

He propped his elbow on the side of the instrument and leaned against it as he regarded her with his head cocked to one side. It was a most un-Darcy-like pose. He was the last man she would expect to drape himself on the furniture.

A moment passed as Elizabeth waited for him to speak.

"I love listening to you play. It is like angels singing," he said finally.

Elizabeth felt her cheeks heat. "I am not that proficient, sir."

He waved away her modesty. "Georgiana wanted me to speak with you."

"Oh?" Elizabeth did not know how else to respond to this non-sequitur.

Leaning forward, he gazed into her eyes with peculiar intensity. "I am in love with you."

Suddenly, Elizabeth was swimming in very deep waters. "I see." She had known this, of course, but had not been prepared for such a naked declaration.

"The question is…do you love me?"

Merciful heavens! Elizabeth had not prepared to declare her sentiments that afternoon. She dropped her eyes to the keyboard. "My sentiments are irrelevant, sir, since nothing can ever happen between us."

He swiftly crossed the space between them and caught one of her hands in his. "Do not say that! I have not given up hope!"

This close, Elizabeth could smell the brandy on his breath. No wonder he was acting so strangely. He might not be foxed, but the spirits were clearly affecting his behavior.

He gazed very intently into her eyes, giving her an opportunity to notice how blue his were—like the summer sky after a storm. *Why am I waxing poetic about his eyes?*

"If this scandal did not stand between us, would you have accepted my offer? Would you accept my offer if I renewed it?" he asked.

Good Lord. What a question! Her feelings about Mr. Darcy were so tangled and confused that she could not begin to answer the question for herself. At one time she would have given him a definite "no," but now… Elizabeth swallowed. "I do not know, sir."

Mr. Darcy released her hand, slumping back against the pianoforte. "You do not know? So perhaps you might refuse me despite—?" He broke off as he ran a hand through already disheveled hair. "Might I know the cause of your hesitation?"

The back of her neck perspired, causing the collar of her dress to stick to her skin. This was the very last conversation she wished to have with this man, but she owed him the truth. "I hold you in great esteem, and I am grateful for all the care you have shown me."

He waved this away. "Yes, so you said before. And yet…"

She took a deep breath. "And yet…I do not know if you could be truly happy with someone from my family background—someone with no name to speak of or lineage of distinction."

He shook his head vigorously and stopped, appearing a little green. "That did concern me at first, but it no longer bothers me. It is your family's *behavior* that I find so abhorrent."

Apparently the Mr. Darcy Elizabeth had met during his first visit to Hertfordshire had not completely disappeared. "Abhorrent?" she repeated.

He stood up straight as though he needed to face her down. "Y-your sisters chase after soldiers, and your mother complains incessantly about her nerves. They show a want of propriety—"

Elizabeth's pulse pounded in her ears. Why did she even attempt to speak with Mr. Darcy? The man was insufferable! "They are my *family*."

"And they have treated you abominably throughout this entire affair with Lord Henry." He waved his arms about wildly. "At Longbourn I wanted to take your mother by the shoulders and shake her. She does not believe you when you are so obviously speaking the truth! And she shows no appreciation for your unique and special qualities." He leaned forward over the top of the pianoforte until he was almost close enough to kiss. "She believes you are simply another girl from Hertfordshire—which you most affirmatively are not."

Elizabeth gaped at him. Was that truly how he saw her? But there was no reason to doubt it. *In vino veritas.*

His defense of her honor warmed her heart, but it was still important to make him understand. "And yet they are my *family*," she said. He frowned at this declaration. "I *love* them."

He regarded her with narrowed eyes and a puzzled expression.

She sighed, considering how to explain it. "Has nobody in your family ever let you down or embarrassed you?" she asked. "Yet you love them still?" Her words seemed to strike him forcefully; he rubbed his mouth as he considered.

She continued, "I cannot cut myself off from my family, no matter their behavior. They are not at their best now, it is true, but someday they may feel differently. I could not bear to lose them."

Mr. Darcy blinked several times, gazing down at the fine-grained wood of the instrument. "Of course. I did not think of it in those terms. I would be loath to give up any of my family…even when they vex me."

Elizabeth sighed with relief. Truthfully, she had not expected him to understand.

"My family certainly has its share of…eccentrics," he continued slowly. "I can hardly begrudge your family their peculiarities while tolerating those among my relatives." He stared at his hands with an almost melancholy expression.

With Mr. Darcy in such subdued spirits, Elizabeth had an odd impulse to comfort him.

His eyes were upon her again. "Do you think you could ever love me?" His voice was rather plaintive. Suddenly, Elizabeth hated the brandy that had so effectively stripped Mr. Darcy of his defenses; he should not be so naked before her.

"Now is not the time to discuss such matters," she insisted. "Not when you are in your cups."

He did not deny it, but his eyes remained fixed on her face, pleading silently. "I pray you, tell me *something*. Give me some cause for hope."

She swallowed hard. "Do not ask me such a question, I beg of you. It will only make it more difficult for me to leave."

Oddly enough, one corner of his mouth curled upward. "It will be difficult for you to leave?"

She owed him the truth. "Very difficult."

"Hmm." He grinned. "I shall take that. For now." And with that, he turned and made his way rather unsteadily from the room.

I shall never understand that man.

***

The three inhabitants of Darcy House enjoyed their idyll for more than a week. Elizabeth was very much improved, but she was still weak and required frequent rests. A wracking cough persisted, and she had not regained the weight she had lost. Mr. Darcy never spoke of their conversation in the music room, but when he spoke of her family, his comments were far more moderate—suggesting that he did recall the conversation that had taken place while he was foxed.

Her own feelings about Mr. Darcy were muddled, and she often found herself attempting to tease them out. Then she would recall that her sentiments about the man did not signify; they could not marry anyway. It was strange. Each time she told herself that, her spirits grew a little more depressed.

And then they faced the arrival of the unexpected guest that Elizabeth had feared.

Elizabeth and Mr. Darcy had been listening to Georgiana play a new piece in the music room. Entranced by the joys of Mozart, Elizabeth realized she had been staring at—and admiring—Mr. Darcy's profile. Fortunately, his eyes were fixed on his sister, and he did not notice. Although she knew it was tempting fate, Elizabeth took the opportunity presented by an unguarded moment to study his face in more detail. He was, of course, a handsome man: dark-haired and tall—features Elizabeth particularly appreciated.

Many people who observed him at that moment would say his face revealed nothing. Elizabeth herself would have made that claim a week ago, but she knew him more intimately now and saw details that would have escaped her before. He was relaxed, enjoying the music. Despite his excessively straight posture, his face did not have the sternness she saw so often. His mouth was soft, relaxed, almost smiling. She loved his eyes and thought his nose was quite patrician. But she positively adored his mouth, a perfect Cupid's bow shape with full, soft-looking lips. What would those lips feel like on hers? What scent would he give off if they were that close? How would his skin feel if she touched it?

The music abruptly fell silent; Elizabeth had heard barely a note. Darcy applauded his sister with a smile, and Elizabeth hastily joined in. *Why am I admiring Mr. Darcy? True, he has been very kind, but soon I must leave Darcy House forever. I cannot grow attached to him when there is no future for us. Not that I want one, of course.*

Mr. Darcy's gaze focused on her face, and she struggled not to smile simply because his eyes were upon her. *I am not a silly schoolgirl.* Instead, she returned his gaze rather blankly. He blinked and frowned, then asked, "Miss Elizabeth, would you grace us with a perf—"

A new—and rather loud—voice floated into the music room through the open door to the front hall. Elizabeth froze; she could never forget that nasal tone.

"Oh, no need to announce me, Greenwood! I am practically a member of the family. The music room, you say?"

Georgiana stared at Elizabeth, stricken. Darcy stood so abruptly that his chair fell over. "Miss Bingley!" he whispered.

Chapter Twelve

Elizabeth looked about for a place to hide but saw only one option. The far end of the room was decorated with a thick set of red velvet curtains, which—being rarely drawn— were swept to one side of the window where the bottom edges pooled on the floor.

Mr. Darcy nodded his approval as Elizabeth slipped behind them, pressing herself back against the wall so the fabric would not bulge noticeably. She had not been overly hasty, for Miss Bingley sailed—with a frantic Mrs. Greenwood behind her—into the room only seconds after Elizabeth disappeared. A worn patch in one fold of the curtain gave Elizabeth a small window through which she could view the room.

Miss Bingley's greetings to Georgiana and Mr. Darcy were unnecessarily effusive. She kissed Georgiana on both cheeks and gave her a bouquet of roses. After exchanging greetings with Mr. Darcy, she sat beside him on the love seat despite the plethora of empty chairs. Was Elizabeth the only one who noticed that he slid closer to the arm of the love seat?

"La! The knocker has been gone from your door for many days!" she exclaimed. "You will cause quite a scandal if you do not receive visitors soon. Have you been unwell?"

"No—" Mr. Darcy started to say.

"Yes," Georgiana exclaimed. "William is too kind, but the truth is that I have had a series of sick headaches and really could not endure any kind of noise. Today is the first day I have been out of my room." She clutched her forehead dramatically. Elizabeth stifled a laugh; Georgiana's act was perfect.

"Oh, how shocking!" Miss Bingley exclaimed. "I do so dislike having a headache. Louisa hates it as well. In fact, most people I have discussed the subject with are remarkably opposed to headaches."

"Imagine the coincidence," Mr. Darcy remarked dryly.

Their guest chattered on, oblivious to his sarcasm. "Of course, I take care that I do not contract them frequently. Having frequent headaches shows a lack of discipline, I believe." Georgiana's eyebrows rose. "Though not in your case, of course, my dear," Miss Bingley added hastily.

Mr. Darcy nodded solemnly. "Georgiana's headaches are always very well disciplined."

Mrs. Greenwood entered with a tray of teacups and biscuits. As she set them down on the table, her eyes ranged around the room, no doubt wondering where their houseguest had gone. Her mouth curled up briefly when her gaze settled on the curtains. At least Elizabeth was providing entertainment for the staff.

Several minutes passed as Mr. Darcy, Miss Bingley, and Georgiana spoke of the weather and mutual acquaintances in London. Then Miss Bingley turned to Georgiana, practically thrusting the bouquet under her nose. "Do you like the fragrance of these flowers? I asked the man for particularly fragrant roses."

Georgiana immediately sneezed. "Roses make me—" Her next words were drowned out by an explosive sneeze.

Miss Bingley's brows knit together. "I am sorry, my dear. What did you say?" Was that a triumphant gleam in her eye?

"Roses make me sneeze," Georgiana said quickly before being cut off by another series of sneezes.

Miss Bingley's mouth formed a perfect "o." "I had no idea. How terribly unfortunate."

Elizabeth fumed silently behind the curtain. She did not know Miss Bingley's purpose, but she knew the woman lied.

Turning bright red with embarrassment, Georgiana rushed to the door. "Please excuse me," she murmured in between sneezes.

The wary look in Mr. Darcy's eyes suggested that he was also suspicious of Miss Bingley's actions. He stood. "I should help Georgiana."

Miss Bingley arose as well, but she placed her hand on Mr. Darcy's shoulder. Behind the curtain, Elizabeth gasped at the woman's impertinence. "Please do not leave right away," Miss Bingley purred. "We so rarely have time alone."

Mr. Darcy plucked the offending hand off his shoulder and allowed it to fall. "This is not seemly, Miss Bingley."

Having received that response, Elizabeth would have fled the room in mortification, but Miss Bingley stepped closer to her quarry. Her fingers entwined themselves in Mr. Darcy's cravat, pulling at the many loops. "I think you would be so much more comfortable without this…"

"Please!" Mr. Darcy lifted her hand from his cravat. Elizabeth considered whether she should reveal herself, but the idea was laughable. Mr. Darcy was a wealthy man of eight and twenty; he hardly needed Elizabeth Bennet to protect him.

Miss Bingley started removing her hair pins so that her elaborate coiffure tumbled down around her shoulders, making her seem quite wanton. Elizabeth's ire grew. How dare she treat Mr. Darcy in such a way—seeking to entrap him into marriage? It would not work. It could not.

Although Mr. Darcy had to marry somebody. What if he decided Miss Bingley was as good a choice as any now that Elizabeth had declined his offer? Goosebumps broke out over Elizabeth's arms. What a horrible thought. He could not marry another woman. He could only marry—

"Miss Bingley!" Mr. Darcy exclaimed. "You cannot—you must put up your hair at once! What if someone were to enter—?" He stood halfway between the door and his guest, unsure of what to do.

Now the woman was undoing the buttons on her bodice and pulling her chemise down to reveal— *Oh, merciful heavens!* Elizabeth thought. *She might actually expose herself to Mr. Darcy! Perhaps I should reveal my presence. Mr. Darcy might need rescuing after all.* It also would offer the advantage of allowing Elizabeth to slap Miss Bingley.

At that moment, another, deeper voice called "Darcy?" from the hallway. This only provided a second's warning before the door was swung open to reveal…

Mr. Bingley.

Instantly, Elizabeth understood the whole of Miss Bingley's scheme. The grim expression on Mr. Darcy's face suggested that he did as well. Knowing that her brother was on his way to Darcy House, Miss Bingley had arranged a tableau which suggested that Mr. Darcy had ravished her.

Mr. Bingley's eager grin immediately transformed to shock as he surveyed the scene before him. While he stood frozen on the threshold, Miss Bingley rushed to him, throwing herself into her brother's arms. "Charles! Thank God you have come. Mr. Darcy has compromised me!"

Mr. Darcy's face had turned bright red. "I have done nothing of the sort," he exclaimed. "Your sister took down her hair and unbuttoned her dress!"

Mr. Bingley looked sadly at his friend while he grappled with the (apparently) sobbing woman clinging to his arms. "Darcy, you know how this looks…" He shrugged apologetically.

The time had come. Elizabeth could not preserve her reputation at the expense of Mr. Darcy's happiness. She would not allow him to be forced into an unhappy union.

While everyone's attention was focused on Miss Bingley at the other side of the room, Elizabeth hastily pushed the curtain aside, slipped out, and seated herself in a nearby chair, affecting a languid pose as if she had been there for quite a while. "It happened just as Mr. Darcy recounted," she said, flipping open her fan.

Miss Bingley gave a violent start.

Mr. Bingley's mouth dropped open. "M-Miss Bennet! I-I did not see you there!"

She smiled at him. "Understandable, given the sight that greeted you upon entering the room."

"Charles!" Miss Bingley screeched, pointing her finger at Elizabeth. "She was not here! She was not present in the room when Mr. D-Darcy took advantage."

Elizabeth laughed, covering her mouth daintily. Mr. Bingley laughed as well. "Not present in the room?" he asked his sister. "Where did she come from, then? There is only one door."

Mr. Bingley released his sister, who scrambled quickly to avoid falling to the floor. He gave Elizabeth a precise bow. "Miss Bennet. A pleasure to see you."

This was like something from a dream. Elizabeth curtseyed as if they were meeting under something resembling ordinary circumstances.

Miss Bingley had taken a chair and was hastily fastening her clothes.

"Bingley," Mr. Darcy said, "you know I would never touch your sister, particularly not with Miss Bennet in the room." He gestured to Elizabeth.

"Of course not." Mr. Bingley turned to his sister. "Caroline, Darcy would hardly compromise you with Miss Bennet in the room. He is not planning to start a harem!" He laughed at his own joke, but nobody joined him. He turned back to Mr. Darcy. "I apologize, Darcy. Sometimes she has a bit of an…overactive imagination."

Miss Bingley stamped her foot. "It was not my imagination!"

Mr. Bingley gave his sister a stern look. "Caroline, the less said, the better."

But now Miss Bingley was staring furiously at Elizabeth. "What is she doing here?"

A muscle twitched in Mr. Darcy's jaw, but his tone remained calm. "She is a guest at Darcy House as she recovers from an illness."

"Oh, is she?" Miss Bingley sneered. "After her infamous behavior in Hertfordshire, I can only imagine what she schemes to do at Darcy House."

Mr. Darcy spoke through gritted teeth. "Her *scheme* is to recuperate from a potentially deadly illness."

Miss Bingley laughed harshly while the others merely stared at her.

Mr. Bingley sighed and shook his head. "Caroline, I believe it is time you went to visit Aunt Agnes in Liverpool. I do not believe the London air agrees with you."

"No!" she cried. "I shall not go to Aunt Agnes." Miss Bingley's expression was mulish.

Mr. Bingley rolled his eyes. "Do you want to suffer additional diminishment of your dress budget?"

The woman gasped as if he had suggested drowning her kitten. "You would not—"

"Not if you go to Liverpool."

"But I do not like Liverpool!" she wailed.

Mr. Bingley took his sister by the elbow and pulled her toward the door, giving Mr. Darcy an apologetic look. "I am terribly sorry about this, Darcy. Perhaps she should not leave the house without a keeper." Miss Bingley made an indignant noise, but her brother ignored it.

"No matter, Bingley," Mr. Darcy replied. "However, it is important that nobody know of Miss Bennet's presence here. She is in…a difficult situation."

"I understand." Mr. Bingley nodded. "You can be assured of my silence *and* my sister's. After all, we are interested in remaining on good terms with the Darcy family, are we not?" He gave his sister a pointed look.

Miss Bingley gave Mr. Darcy a tight-lipped smile. "Naturally."

"I am certain Mr. Darcy is grateful for your cooperation," Mr. Bingley said as he pushed his sister through the doorway. "Darcy, I shall see you at the club."

Mr. Darcy waved to his friend, and then the Bingleys disappeared from sight.

"I do not want to visit Aunt Agnes!" Miss Bingley's voice wailed from the hallway. "This is not my fault! I did nothing…" Her voice faded as her brother drew her further from the music room. Finally, the front door closed with an audible click.

Just then Georgiana walked back into the music room with a red nose and a handkerchief still in her hand. "What happened to Miss Bingley? Has she left already?"

"Indeed, she has," Mr. Darcy intoned solemnly, but Elizabeth saw a hint of amusement glinting in his eye.

She could contain it no longer. She burst into laughter. After a moment, Mr. Darcy joined in.

***

The next day Mr. Darcy was at breakfast when Elizabeth joined him. After exchanging greetings, she helped herself to some eggs, toast, and ham at the sideboard and seated herself across the table from him. He watched her surreptitiously as she spread butter on her toast. Her lips were pursed in concentration, and wisps of dark curly hair fell over her face. He had never seen anything so charming. She took a delicate bite of toast, and Darcy nearly choked on his bite of eggs. How could something so simple be so alluring?

He should stop staring, but he was mesmerized. A crumb clung to her upper lip until the tip of her pink tongue wiped it away. She took another bite, and Darcy found himself hoping for another crumb.

When had it grown so blasted hot in the breakfast room? Darcy set down his knife and took a deep breath. Finally wrenching his gaze from Elizabeth's mouth, he stared at his plate, attempting to get his wayward feelings under control.

She is a guest in my house. I cannot do anything that might take advantage of her.

I wonder what it would be like to kiss those lips.

After everything that had transpired during her illness, Darcy felt closer to her than ever before, but what if she did not? Perhaps she was eager to escape Darcy House and its inhabitants.

He was startled by the sound of Elizabeth clearing her throat. "Mr. Darcy, as Miss Bingley's visit shows quite plainly, I cannot remain at Darcy House."

"I would say your presence proved extremely beneficial yesterday," he drawled with a smile.

She did not return it. "It is unlikely that other visitors will be so easily silenced, and I do not want to be responsible for your family's loss of reputation."

"That does not concern me," Darcy responded immediately.

"It concerns me!" Elizabeth said with some asperity. "I am in London to spare my family the pain of sharing in my disgrace. It was not my intention to transfer that liability to your family."

Darcy was chagrined. "I did not mean to make light of your situation."

"You have been most gracious hosts, but the longer I remain, the greater the danger of being discovered." She pressed her lips together in a thin line. "I do not want you to suffer because of your kindness to me."

Darcy's entire body tensed. The moment he had been dreading was upon him. She was threatening to leave, and yet her feelings remained a mystery. He considered asking again, but he was likely to receive the same response. "Where would you go?"

Her eyes were focused on her fork as she speared bits of egg on her plate. "I will look for a boarding house—hopefully with a landlady who is more responsible." After a pause, she added, "I have some money from my father, and I had been seeking a position in a shop. I should be able to secure employment soon." The slight tremor in her voice suggested that she was not as sure of her words as she would like to appear.

Darcy could not prevent his shudder. He had known it was probable she had sought employment, but a position as a shop girl? In what sort of shop? The idea was fraught with danger, bringing to mind every newspaper story about crime in London. He imagined her walking out of the door to live in a stranger's house and work in some shabby shop. He could not stomach it.

To hell with ascertaining her feelings; he could do that later. He had to prevent this insanity and find some way to secure her safety. Gripping the edge of the table with both hands, he spoke in a low growl, "Elizabeth, I would like you to stay here indefinitely. Or forever. I would still dearly love to make you my wife."

Her eyes widened, but he knew her response as soon as she lowered her gaze to the tablecloth. "I thank you for the honor, sir"—Darcy was beginning to hate that phrase —"but nothing about my situation has changed in the least. I am not in a position to accept an offer of marriage from anyone." Were her hands trembling as she grasped her fork? Darcy would like to think that it was more difficult for her to refuse him a second time. She set the fork down beside her plate. "And it would be best if I leave immediately, before I am discovered at Darcy House."

If Elizabeth were found at Darcy House, it would be assumed that he had compromised her reputation, and they would be forced into marriage. The prospect was not unattractive in the least. He would be grateful to anything that would convince her to accept his offer—even such monumental embarrassment. However, it would come at the price of further damage to *her* reputation, when her self-esteem was already quite battered. He could not wish that upon her.

He dared to reach across the table and take her hand. She did not resist. Perhaps she was not indifferent to him after all. "I do not care, nor does Georgiana. She would love to call you sister."

"I cannot allow you to make such a sacrifice for my sake."

He made a harsh noise at the back of his throat. "I pray you, reconsider."

She shook her head. "As long as this stigma clings to my reputation, I cannot consider marrying any honorable man."

Darcy needed to move. Pushing back his chair, he stood and stalked the length of the breakfast room and back. Elizabeth watched, bemused. He felt as helpless and as angry as he had at the side of her sickbed. At least this time she was awake.

"I have done everything possible to save your life—" he started.

"And I am most grateful," Elizabeth interjected.

"But now you would toss it all away!" he exclaimed. "You will leave for an unknown position in an unknown part of the city, and I will never know if you are safe or if you are well. It seems a paltry way to repay my efforts."

Elizabeth's face went blank. She placed her napkin upon the table and slowly rose to her feet. "Are you saying, sir, that my life now belongs to you? You saved my life, and now I am yours to command?"

The blood drained from Darcy's face. "Lord, no," he murmured. "I am not *that* man. I am not like that-that *viscount*!" He spat the name like an epithet.

Elizabeth clutched the back of her chair. "I do not see a difference in kind, only in degree."

He took a deep breath; now was not the time to give free rein to his temper. "You do not know what it was like seeing you on that cot in the boarding house." His voice cracked with emotion. "For a moment I feared I had arrived too late, but then you took a breath—and breathed hope back into my life. I vowed to do anything in my power to ensure that you lived."

Her lips were slightly parted as she listened. "I-I am sorry. I did not know…"

He continued. "I cannot leave you to the good offices of the people of London. Every day I would worry about where you were and what was happening to you."

Elizabeth closed her eyes for a moment. When she opened them, they stared into the middle distance, focused on nothing. "I cannot be held prisoner by your anxiety any more than I can be subject to Lord Henry's desire for me."

Oh, Good Lord, is that what I am asking of her? Darcy felt a sharp pang of guilt; he could not expect her to live her life for him. He would not want her to. "No, of course not," he said.

"Then it seems we are at an impasse, which can only be resolved by my removal."

"Wait." With the threat of her departure looming over him, Darcy had expected the familiar despair to descend upon him, but something in her manner suggested that she wished she could accept his offer. If there was some cause for hope.

No, Darcy decided. There *was* cause for hope. He would not accept her refusal as final. An idea was taking shape in Darcy's mind. "But what if your reputation were changed? For the better?"

She smiled sadly at him. "Once a woman's reputation is lost, it is lost forever."

Excitement built in Darcy's chest. "But not if we can prove that he lied about your loss of reputation."

She avoided his eyes. "He and I were the only ones in the room that evening. No one will believe me. No one *does* believe me save you, Jane, and my father."

"There must be some way to let the truth be known." Elizabeth shrugged helplessly. "I will investigate it." He resumed his seat, eyeing what remained of his breakfast.

"I must still leave Darcy House," Elizabeth said hastily.

Darcy's head jerked up. "You shall reside at Darcy House until this matter is resolved," he said simply. Had he not made that clear?

"Mr. Darcy, I am not a member of your staff, to be ordered about," she sighed. "And I cannot remain here."

Darcy could only imagine the joy he would experience with Elizabeth in residence indefinitely. "Why not?"

One of her brows lifted as she regarded him. "Imagine that you do manage to repair my reputation by some feat of magic. It will not matter one whit if anyone discovers we have been living under the same roof without a proper chaperone."

Darcy grimaced; he was neatly caught with his own logic. He pushed his empty plate away and folded his hands on the table. Did she not understand his concern about her safety? "I will never rest easy if I do not know where you are and if you are safe."

Tipping her head to the side, she gave him a half smile. "Surely you will learn to live with the uncertainty."

He leaned forward in his seat, not taking his eyes from hers. "I am in love with you, Miss Elizabeth. I will *never* overcome my concern for your wellbeing."

She swallowed, staring down at her plate. "I apologize, sir. It was not my intention to cause you any pain."

Had he reacted too harshly? But he also felt a pang of sadness. Surely if she felt a glimmering of love for him, she would have responded in kind. Would she not? He banished these bleak thoughts. It did not matter. She was no less worthy of his assistance if she did not return his feelings.

Elizabeth took a deep breath and dissolved into a fit of coughing. Such episodes were disturbing and did not appear to be decreasing in frequency; however, Dr. Hanson had assured Darcy that they should abate eventually.

Darcy took her hand. "Elizabeth, do you believe you should go to live in another boarding house when your health is still uncertain? You tire easily and are prone to coughing. You should not be on your own."

Elizabeth sat, folding her hands before her on the table. "I suppose that point is irrefutable," she conceded. "However, it seems we have reached a stalemate. I do not want to ruin any reputations by remaining here, and you do not want to risk my safety somewhere else. Perhaps we could reach a compromise. Perhaps there is room in your stable?" A corner of her mouth quirked upward.

Darcy chuckled, but the suggestion had sparked an idea. "I have a property," he said slowly. "A small house on Charles Street, not far from here. Usually it is available for lease, but at the moment it stands empty. Would you do me the honor of taking up residence there temporarily? You could recover. I would know you are safe, and you would not be required to seek immediate employment."

She frowned at him. "How do you come to have such a house?"

Darcy felt his face heat. "I inherited it from my father. He…umm…" Darcy cleared his throat. "He kept his mistress there. He took up with her only after my mother passed away. I knew nothing of it until after his death. I intended to allow the woman to live there permanently, but she found a new…er…patron and moved out. It has been leased to tenants since then." No doubt his face was quite red. He had never expected to discuss such a subject with a lady.

"Oh." Elizabeth's face was flushed as well. He would understand if she declined the offer simply based on the house's provenance. Elizabeth pursed her lips and frowned, staring out of the window behind him. Finally, she said, "I will accept your offer"—Darcy's whole body sagged in relief —"temporarily and upon one condition: you allow me to repay the rent once I find employment."

"That is not necessary."

"I insist."

He shook his head. "You are a difficult woman to help." She shrugged and gave him a helpless smile. Darcy had no intention of accepting a penny from Elizabeth, but they had finally arrived at a fragile truce. "Very well."

Elizabeth relaxed against the back of her chair. "When can I take up residency?" she asked.

His whole body tightened at the thought that she would no longer be under his roof. "The house is available now, but it will need airing and preparation for a new resident," he responded. "Perhaps you can remain for one more night to take dinner with me and Georgiana?"

She hesitated for a moment. "Very well."

Was her grim expression because she wanted to leave Darcy House earlier or because she feared for her hosts' reputations? He wished he knew.

Chapter Thirteen

The following morning Elizabeth walked to her new home with Emily, one of the Darcy House maids. The tradition was to call maids by their surnames, but Elizabeth preferred to be on friendlier terms with the servants, and so had asked if Emily minded being called by her Christian name. Mr. Darcy wanted to deliver Elizabeth to the small house in his carriage, but Elizabeth had no desire to make her arrival so conspicuous. And it was only a walk of ten minutes.

Having been cooped up in Darcy House for more than a week, she found it was quite pleasant to be outside again. The March air held a chill, but Elizabeth relished the cold after so many days indoors. The sky was clear, a bright blue, and the sun warmed her face.

They finally arrived at Charles Street, which was in a pleasant enough neighborhood, although not quite as fashionable as Darcy House. However, Elizabeth had resigned herself to the fact that she could not venture out of the house very often lest she encounter an acquaintance. Fortunately, Mr. Darcy had assured her that the house had a large back garden.

The house was indeed small, squeezed between two larger townhouses near the end of the street. It had two bedrooms upstairs and a kitchen and sitting room downstairs. A little room off the kitchen would be Emily's bedroom.

Elizabeth explored the house quickly and then sought out the garden. As promised, it was quite a bit bigger than what would be expected from a house of this size. It was surrounded by tall brick walls, providing quite a bit of privacy. The garden itself had been well tended, with several shady trees, a few benches, and neat beds of flowers.

Finished with her perusal, Elizabeth reentered the house. A footman had arrived by dog cart; he and Emily were carrying Elizabeth's trunk upstairs. The inside of the house was pleasant, with cheerful yellow wallpaper and lace curtains. Certainly nothing about it cried out that it was a "haven for sin" built for a wealthy man's mistress. Elizabeth laughed at her own preconceptions. The old Mr. Darcy's mistress was likely quite an ordinary woman making the best of her lot in life.

She seated herself on a somewhat worn loveseat. It would be a relief not to face concerns about rent or landladies—or to look for employment immediately. Yet she could not prevent a nagging feeling of anxiety. It was improper to accept such largess from an unmarried man, although, truthfully, Elizabeth had done so many improper things recently that she was becoming somewhat accustomed to it.

On the other hand, she did not like feeling beholden to Mr. Darcy—or the uncertainty about how long the arrangement would last. Certainly she could not live here indefinitely, like a poor, exiled relation of the Darcy family. Mr. Darcy seemed to think that something about her situation would change, and somehow they could erase the stain from her reputation, but Elizabeth had given up hope of miracles long ago.

And if she was honest with herself, she was uneasy because the arrangement made her feel like a kept woman. She knew Mr. Darcy's sole motivation was ensuring her safety, and he would not make improper demands, but the circumstances still felt quite illicit. Upon learning of such an arrangement, almost anybody would assume Mr. Darcy was taking her to his bed.

Elizabeth buried her head in her hands. Had she made a mistake? As she knew very well, the appearance of immorality was just as bad as immorality itself. She might as well be his mistress; he was supporting her as if she were.

Then she laughed at herself. She was thinking like the Elizabeth Bennet who had a reputation to protect, but that woman no longer existed. Perhaps it was time to cease worrying about what people thought of her virtue. Yet she seemed incapable of not caring; apparently she did have a remaining shred of pride after all. Perhaps it was honor, as Mr. Darcy would say—what she knew to be true about herself. Or perhaps the old Elizabeth Bennet of Longbourn still lurked inside her weary body.

The footman thudded down the stairs and disappeared through the door with a nod to her. "Miss?" Emily descended the stairs more circumspectly, watching Elizabeth with concern. Elizabeth lifted her head, hoping her eyes were not too red.

"I am simply fatigued," Elizabeth said. "Nothing is amiss." *Except for my loss of reputation—and the rest of my life.*

***

Darcy managed to delay visiting Elizabeth in her new house for sixteen whole hours, but by the following morning he was forced to surrender to his overwhelming curiosity and (he had to admit) desire for her company. She drew him like iron to a magnet. The knowledge that she was a short walk away and nearly alone in his house enticed him in ways he had not anticipated.

Elizabeth herself answered his knock and appeared quite startled to see him. Did she really believe he could stay away? "Mr. Darcy!"

"May I come in for a few minutes?" he asked.

She gave an uncertain laugh. "It is your house."

Darcy scowled. "Not now. For now it is your house, and I would not enter without your permission."

She stepped away from the doorway and gestured expansively toward the drawing room. "Please come in."

He hung his greatcoat and hat on hooks near the door and walked into the drawing room. He had been here before, of course. But there was something about Elizabeth's presence that caused him to feel like a big, clumsy man intruding on a delicate feminine world. Perhaps it was because he was so tall, and the drawing room was so small. Elizabeth gestured to a loveseat. "I pray you, be seated."

Darcy sat, noting that the upholstery was a bit frayed. That was unacceptable; he must have it replaced. Elizabeth took the chair opposite the loveseat. After an acutely awkward pause, she said, "I can make some tea if you would like."

Darcy's eyebrows shot up. "Surely Emily can do that?"

Elizabeth smoothed her skirts. "Her mother is sick, so I gave her the day off to go visit her."

"The whole day?" Darcy asked in disbelief. He could not imagine Georgiana living without servants for an entire day.

Elizabeth laughed. "Such a small house does not require much care. I am quite capable of fending for myself."

Darcy reminded himself that Elizabeth had lived alone in a boarding house for almost two weeks. Of course, she had nearly died, but that was not from her own incompetence. "But what about food?" he asked, somewhat alarmed. "Surely—"

She sighed. "Alas, I am completely inept when it comes to matters of the kitchen, but Emily has left me some ham and bread. I am hoping she will teach me to cook."

"Cook?" Darcy said more loudly than he intended. "Why?"

She regarded him steadily. "My future may very well not include a household with servants. I must learn to do for myself."

A fist tightened around Darcy's heart. He knew she had no intention of accepting his proposal, but such statements reminded him forcefully. "It does not have to be that way."

"Yes, it does."

He wondered what it cost her to hold herself so still and controlled.

Darcy's walking stick fell from where he had propped it by the loveseat, clattering to the floor with a noise that echoed throughout the mostly empty house. Elizabeth startled at the sound.

Elizabeth and I are alone, Darcy realized with a growing sense of wonder. He had expected the presence of the maid to act as a chaperone, but here they were *alone* in a comfortable house, enjoying complete privacy. Just as quickly, he pushed those thoughts away. *I cannot yield to temptation. Elizabeth relies on my behavior as a gentleman. I do not want her to think me little better than Lord Henry.*

Another awkward silence followed. The color rose in her cheeks in response to his attention; she shifted uneasily in her chair and directed her gaze to the fireplace. She *did not forget we are alone.*

I am staring at her. But he could not drag his eyes away.

The delicate blush only added to her charms, particularly when set off by her pale green muslin gown. The dress itself was nothing special, neither elegant nor daringly revealing. Yet there was something so enticing about it. The fabric clung to her legs. A fichu in the bodice covered her upper chest, but Darcy could easily imagine what he would see if she removed it. The creamy skin of her neck and the delicate swell of her—

"Biscuits!" Darcy said the first thing that came to mind as he tore his eyes from her form. Elizabeth's brows drew together in perplexity. "Er…perhaps some biscuits?" he suggested, locking his gaze on a painting of a sailing ship beside the window.

Elizabeth rushed to her feet. "I believe we may have some lemon biscuits," she said quickly. "Cook sent Emily with such a large hamper of food one would think we were going on an expedition into the wilderness."

Darcy laughed at her joke, as relieved as she was to have a new subject for conversation.

"I pray you, excuse me." Her heels tapped on the floor as she strode toward the kitchen.

In her absence, Darcy scrubbed both hands over his face. "Get ahold of yourself, Darcy," he ordered himself in a low voice. As always,

Elizabeth tempted him every moment of every day. However, Darcy House teemed with people who might burst in on them at any moment, serving as an effective check on his ardor. Here he was in far more danger…

He heard a clatter and a dull thud. Darcy was out of his chair in a heartbeat and striding into the kitchen. He found Elizabeth bending over to retrieve something from the floor, presenting a very nice view of her—

He dragged his eyes away to focus on the fascinating masonry of the kitchen fireplace. "Are you hurt, Eliz—Miss Elizabeth?"

She stood with a rueful smile on her lips. "I am afraid I am a bit of a menace in the kitchen right now. I managed to knock both the cutting board and the knife onto the floor." She replaced the objects on the nearby table.

He examined her from head to toe. "But you are uninjured?"

"Yes. I managed to stay safe from flying cutting boards." She laughed softly.

He loved the sound of her laughter, which was far lower than her speaking voice and not at all like the high-pitched tittering of the ladies of the *ton*. Somehow her laugh managed to convey far more joy than anything produced by any woman at any ball he had ever attended. How was that possible?

His gaze rose from her neck to her lips to her eyes, which happened to be peering right into his. How long did they stand, eyes locked, gazing into each other's souls? "Elizabeth…" he breathed. In that moment he felt they were in perfect accord. Or was that an illusion fostered by his wishful imagination?

She spun toward the table. "Biscuits. I know the basket is around here—ah!" She retrieved a large basket from the floor and placed it on the table. Opening a cabinet, she pulled down a plate and hastily filled it with biscuits, which she then thrust at him with a forced smile. "There! They do look delicious."

Darcy's eyes had no interest in the biscuits. They refused to look anywhere but at Elizabeth's mouth. He took a step toward her. Her eyes widened, but she did not retreat. Another step. Only a few inches separated them now.

One hand snaked behind her head, the other pulled her at the waist, drawing her against his body. Hastily, Elizabeth laid the plate of biscuits on the table, and then her hands were entwined around his waist. As his lips descended to hers, Darcy hesitated for a moment. Did she truly want this? But her eyes were closed, and her face was turned upward, her lips slightly apart. Darcy had never seen a more beautiful sight.

He could not have prevented their kiss at that moment any more than he could have prevented a runaway carriage. Their mouths met forcefully. Her lips were as soft as he had guessed, but he wanted to taste more. When Darcy's tongue sought entry along the seam of Elizabeth's lips, she gave a little gasp of surprise, but her lips parted eagerly. As he explored her mouth, she moaned, a deep sound emanating from the center of her body—and vibrating through his. He pulled her closer until there was no space between them at all.

The hand on her neck traveled down the bare skin and under the edge of her fichu to stroke the soft skin of her back. Her breathing sped up, and she clutched him even more tightly. Lord, she was so beautifully responsive to his every touch! *Why have I denied myself this pleasure for so long?* He was insane to think he could have ever resisted this temptation. His lips never left hers. He was greedy for more. And more. There could never be enough kisses, enough of the taste of Elizabeth on his lips.

One of Elizabeth's hairpins fell from her coiffure onto the kitchen tiles with an audible clatter. Startled, Elizabeth pushed herself away from Darcy, holding him at arms' length. Hot and disheveled, they stood panting and staring at each other. Darcy awaited her signal. If she took a single step toward him, he was prepared to sweep her off her feet.

She shook her head. "We cannot." Her voice was a low mutter as if she spoke as much to herself as to him. "We cannot."

Darcy ran two hands through his already disordered hair. Good Lord, what must she think of him? He had attacked her like a beast! Would she now regard him as she did the viscount? The thought was abhorrent to him. "I apologize, Elizabeth. I did not mean to lose control—"

She had backed against the kitchen table, half leaning on it for support, but she shook her head, waving away his apology.

Darcy was not finished. "Please accept my apology. If you desire my absence, I will—"

"Mr. Darcy!" she interrupted.

"William," he corrected.

She sighed. "Mr. Darcy, I could have slapped you if the kiss was unwanted."

Darcy blinked. "Really? You would have slapped me?"

She laughed. "Do you think me incapable of expressing my disapproval?"

It was a good point. "Er…no."

"Indeed. I have been practicing my slapping in case I encounter another…impertinent gentleman." Was she joking? Darcy did not know.

"And who have you been practicing this delightful new skill on?" he asked.

Her hand flew to her mouth. "I would not slap another person! Well, not an innocent one."

Why am I not surprised? "So *what* have you been practicing it on? Pigs? Horses? Dogs?"

"I would never strike an animal!" she protested. Then she drew herself up. "If you must know, I practiced on pillows."

Darcy tried hard to suppress a smile, but then Elizabeth began laughing at herself, and he could no longer contain his merriment. Laughing together felt good, nearly as intimate as kissing. When the laughter died down, Darcy said, "I hope the pillows in this household are safe from you. I would not want them abused."

She grinned. "They will be safe from my wrath as long as they do not try to kiss me."

The words had a sobering effect on both of them.

"I am sorry," Darcy said. "It was wholly inappropriate and will not happen again."

She stared into space, a muscle tightening in her jaw. "Not even if I want it to?"

Excitement rushed through Darcy's veins, bubbling through his blood, but he carefully kept his voice even. "Would you like me to?"

She touched her lips with a finger in a kind of wonder. "I think I do." Her face turned up toward his. "I have never wanted a man to kiss me before."

When she said such things, Darcy could not restrain himself. His hands, his lips, indeed his whole body was greedy for a touch of her. Reaching out, he enveloped her in his arms and crushed her to his chest. "Elizabeth!" he murmured in her ear. He wanted to hold her forever.

When he finally released her, Elizabeth's eyes were unfocused and a little glassy. "Mr. Darcy, do—"

"For the love of all that is holy!" he exclaimed. "Will you please call me William?"

She smiled, reaching up to smooth some hair behind his ear. "William is the perfect name for you," she said. Darcy held very still as her hand explored his neck. Finally, it rested at the juncture of his neck and shoulder, feeling perfectly natural.

He bent toward her for another kiss but stopped halfway for an even more important matter. "Now will you please marry me?"

"No."

Darcy dropped his hands. How she could kiss him so passionately without agreeing to be his wife? "But—"

Her eyes stared at the far wall. "If circumstances were different…but scandal is still attached to my name, William. I would not have it attached to yours."

He clasped her shoulders. "I would far rather brave scandal than a lifetime without you."

"I"—she swallowed —"I must admit that it grows more and more difficult to imagine saying goodbye to you."

Darcy counted this a small victory. "Will you at least think on it?" he asked. "Consider it? I will not importune you for an answer now, but I pray you, do not dismiss the idea of our future together." He stroked her hair gently; the curls were every bit as soft as he had envisioned. "And I will continue to investigate how we may clear your name."

Her body relaxed under his hands. "Very well, William. I will consider it." He smiled at her. "Why does that earn a smile?" she asked.

"I kissed you."

"Indeed, you did."

Darcy could not stop smiling. "I was recalling a time when I feared I would never have the opportunity to kiss you."

Her face softened. Did she guess what time he meant? "You did not miss your chance. I am here."

Darcy was so pleased by this declaration that nothing would do but that he would kiss her again.

Chapter Fourteen

It had been three long days since Mr. Darcy visited the little house. Elizabeth tried to stay busy. Mr. Darcy had thoughtfully ensured that the residence was thoroughly stocked with books, and she read avidly. But reading could hardly occupy every minute—or every thought.

It was a good thing that he stayed away, she reminded herself. *It was.* He was far too tempting for her peace of mind.

Still, for those moments in the kitchen…their encounter had been magical. The kind of kisses every woman dreamed about.

Do not get your heart set on things you cannot have.

Although she longed for love, Elizabeth had always considered herself to be rather pragmatic. Before that first kiss, she had never really understood how an unmarried young woman could lose all sense and abandon all rational thought because of a man.

Now she understood.

So she was glad he stayed away. She was. Yet she found herself frequently wondering, in those moments when her mind was not otherwise occupied (and sometimes when it should have been), what Mr. Darcy was doing and when he would return to her. No, not to *her*, of course. To the house. For a visit.

At this point in her internal monologue, Elizabeth often sought to distract herself with a book. Or a biscuit.

Today she was attempting distraction in the form of nature. The weather had warmed in the last few days, and buds had appeared on the bushes and trees of the back garden. Crocuses peeked their heads out along the path.

Elizabeth had been reading a book about the history of Italy, which should have been quite interesting but seemed to have been written for the purpose of helping insomniacs achieve slumber. Having abandoned the book, she was simply sitting on the bench, enjoying the sensations of late afternoon sunshine on her face. The new leaves sprouting on the tree above her created a dappled canopy of green.

The house's back door squeaked, and Elizabeth turned in that direction, expecting to see Emily. Instead, Mr. Darcy stepped past the threshold. Elizabeth hurried to her feet. Somehow it did not seem wise to greet Mr. Darcy sitting down.

They exchanged greetings. "I apologize for intruding," Mr. Darcy said. "Emily let me in but then retired to her room. She looked only half awake."

Elizabeth nodded sympathetically. "She took a sleeping draught. The poor girl has a sick headache which worsens in bright light, so a darkened room is best for her."

"I see," Mr. Darcy said slowly.

Good heavens, we are alone together once again! She had expected that when she saw him next, Emily would be present to inhibit any…untoward impulses. Mr. Darcy suddenly took an intense interest in the ivy growing up one wall. Perhaps he had arrived at the same realization.

After a long, uncomfortable silence, he cleared his throat. "I have gathered some useful information about Lord Henry that I would like to share with you." He gestured to the bench. "Shall we sit?"

The garden bench was not large, and sitting placed them in closer proximity than she would have liked. No, Elizabeth was determined to be honest with herself. She very much liked the proximity, but it was closer than what was *wise*. Perhaps Mr. Darcy was affected by their closeness as well; he seemed to forget his purpose once they were seated. Rather than speaking, he stared at her mouth.

She cleared her throat. "You learned something about the viscount?"

Mr. Darcy blinked. "Oh yes. I asked about in my club and inquired from various acquaintances. I also hired an investigator who traveled to Kent." Mr. Darcy hesitated. "Lord Henry is considered charming by many acquaintances, but there are many people who do not care for his company. I believe he has been residing in Hertfordshire to avoid some of the scandals he left behind in Kent."

Elizabeth closed her eyes, hating herself for having fallen into the man's trap.

Mr. Darcy put his finger under her chin and tipped her head up so she would meet his eyes. "You have done nothing wrong."

She gave a harsh laugh. "I was a gullible fool—"

"Elizabeth, most women would have agreed to his offer of marriage. They would not have recognized his trap for what it was. They would not have recognized the viscount for who he truly is."

She nodded, finding her spirits somewhat improved by his words.

"I suspect you attracted his attention precisely because you did not fall for his charms," Mr. Darcy continued. "The viscount apparently enjoys a challenge."

Elizabeth frowned. "A challenge?"

"He likes to persuade an initially reluctant young lady of the virtue of his charms." Darcy chuckled. "Only he did not anticipate how much of a challenge you would be."

His hand gently stroked her cheek. She swallowed. "I thank you for those words. They do help."

"And every single one is true."

"What else did you learn about the viscount?"

"At first the investigator and I found nothing but the expected vices— and those are all too common to be of any use," he said. "However, upon closer inspection, we discovered that in addition to having acquired more mistresses than is generally considered seemly"—Mr. Darcy arched his brow —"he also has extensive gambling debts."

Elizabeth frowned. "I do not see how that would help clear my name."

"It occurred to me that a person who owned some, or all, of those debts would have leverage over Lord Henry."

"Pressuring him to tell the truth about our encounter?"

"Precisely." Mr. Darcy stroked his chin. "I could buy up his debts and force him to tell the truth."

She considered this possibility. "I am not certain that would be sufficient. Even if he recanted publicly, people would doubt, particularly if there was any suspicion he had been coerced."

"But it might be enough."

"Why would Lord Henry change his story suddenly, especially when it paints him as less than truthful?" Elizabeth pointed out. "No, there would always be a cloud of suspicion over any such denial—and thus doubt about my virtue."

Mr. Darcy leaned forward, resting his arms on his knees and staring at the ground. "I suppose you are right." He rubbed a hand over his face. "I would try the scheme if we can find no other recourse. But we will continue to investigate. Surely there is some way the man can be worked on."

Elizabeth did not have such faith, but she nodded in agreement anyway. She and Mr. Darcy came from different worlds. He must have rarely encountered obstacles that could not be surmounted by will, fortune, or rank. Being a woman from an undistinguished family, Elizabeth was not unaccustomed to reaching the limits of her influence. Perhaps she would need to teach Mr. Darcy the art of acceptance.

Beside her, Mr. Darcy straightened up, his arm accidentally brushing against her waist as he leaned toward her. She stifled a gasp. Why was his touch so provoking to her? It was as if it agitated every nerve in her body.

When he turned toward her, all she could see was the dark depths of his eyes. There was pain in those depths, no doubt reflected in her eyes. But she could also see the spark of his passion. There was something about this comingling of pain and love that spurred a realization. *He truly does love me. Mr. Darcy of Pemberley. Mr. Darcy of ten thousand a year, who must be sought by many women. Mr. Darcy loves* me. *It is entirely incredible.*

Her sense of wonder was immediately washed away by the realization that he could not be hers. Mr. Darcy could hope, but she had no faith that they could ever be together. The glories of love were within her reach, but she could not grasp them. Anger surged at Lord Henry, stronger than ever before. He had taken everything else from her. Her home. Her family. Her future. Why must he also take this?

Tearing her eyes from the increasingly painful sight of Mr. Darcy, Elizabeth fixed them on the distant garden wall. She swallowed hard and blinked, but wetness gathered in her eyes, threatening to escape down her cheeks.

"Elizabeth?" Mr. Darcy's voice was as gentle as his comforting touch on her neck. "I am sorry I do not have better news for you."

She shook her head, keeping her eyes focused on the red brick wall as though everything would fall to pieces if she glanced away for even a second. She could never be his wife. In fact, she should relinquish the charade that there was any hope of bettering her lot in life. She should thank Mr. Darcy for his care and take her leave, returning to the business of seeking employment.

Her heart quailed. Not so much at the prospect of looking for a position, but at the idea that she would leave Mr. Darcy behind. Once she departed this little house, she must never have any further contact with him. To fully avoid temptation, she would do best to leave London—a thought that threatened to provoke a fresh round of tears. They would only ever share a handful of kisses, and even those must remain forever secret.

She balled her handkerchief in one hand. The world believed her to be a fallen woman when she was not. *And now I cling stubbornly to my virtue—for what purpose? I am already condemned.*

No wonder Lord Henry thought he could trick her into becoming his mistress. Once her reputation was tarnished, there was nothing to prevent wanton behavior—and nowhere else she could seek help. *Or so he had believed. If it had not been for Mr. Darcy, the viscount's scheme might have worked.* She shuddered at the thought.

Without Mr. Darcy, she might have died of a fever in the boarding house.

And she would repay his kindness by accepting his kisses and then leaving his arms forever. The man who had given her more help during this crisis than anyone…even her own family. Who believed her assertions of innocence without a shred of evidence.

It was enough to make Elizabeth wish she *could* be Mr. Darcy's mistress. Anyone who saw them together in this house would assume that she already was.

I could be his mistress. Why not?

Clinging to a reputation nobody believed was not making her happy. In fact, it had led her directly to the boarding house and an illness which had nearly killed her. If everyone assumed she was Mr. Darcy's mistress, her virtue would not signify anyway. So why should she clasp it to her chest? Why should she condemn herself to a lonely, loveless life because of an incident that was not her fault?

But in the next moment Elizabeth knew she could not do it. Become a rich man's mistress? The shame would be too great. Even if no one else knew, she could not be happy compromising her values in such a way. *Honor is what you know about yourself.*

At that moment her honor might be slightly tarnished by illicit kisses, but it was still intact. She had no reason to be ashamed.

No, she could not give Mr. Darcy her honor, her life. But perhaps she could give him the afternoon…before she left. Then at least she would have a taste of the passion and the love that would be forever barred from her.

Elizabeth did not wish to contemplate her decision overly long or take the chance of changing her mind. She knew it was the right choice.

Her tears had dried; she was calm and clear-eyed as she turned toward Mr. Darcy. Although she knew what she wanted, did she dare ask for it? She had never considered herself particularly forward, especially in matters of the heart. For the first time in her life, she found herself wishing for some of Lydia's boldness. Elizabeth licked dry lips, wondering how to speak her thoughts.

Mr. Darcy's hand was rubbing gentle circles on her back as he watched her with tender concern. "Mr. Darcy," she began. "W-will you...w-will y-you—" she stuttered in frustration. Such subjects were terribly awkward to discuss.

"I will do anything for you, my love," he said, grasping her arms gently and pulling her toward him.

"Will you kiss me?" she said quickly before she lost her nerve.

He chuckled softly. "And here I thought you might request something I would be reluctant to do."

The kiss started soft and languorous, not at all like the urgent need of his previous visit. But as the kiss grew more ardent, Mr. Darcy's actions became more unconstrained. He kissed the delicate skin under her ear, sending shivers all over her body. Then he laid a line of soft kisses down her neck. When he reached the edge of her sleeve, he pushed it aside to kiss the top of her shoulder.

The dress slid down her arm, revealing her chemise. Elizabeth ignored the twinge of unease caused by such immodesty and reveled in the sensations of having her naked skin touched in such unexpected places. Why had she waited so long to feel a man's touch? But then she doubted other men would feel like this. Her head fell back as she relished the sensations.

Suddenly, Mr. Darcy pulled away from her with a hiss. Elizabeth opened her eyes. Had they been discovered? He was staring at her bare shoulder as if he had accidentally stabbed her with a knife. "My love, I am sorry. I did not intend to..." Looking down, Elizabeth saw that everything was covered save her shoulder and upper arm, but Mr. Darcy must have felt he had gone too far. He reached out as if to fix her dress but then hesitated, perhaps unsure if he should touch her at all.

No doubt her smiled appeared half-drugged. "Do not apologize, William. I pray you, continue."

His eyebrows shot up his forehead. "No, if I continue, I will—you cannot test my self-control like this. I would not act like a gentleman."

She touched her fingers to the curls at the back of his head; his breathing turned ragged. "I do not want your self-control." With her other hand, she played with the starched fabric of his cravat, a bit amazed at her own boldness.

"Good Lord, Elizabeth!" William pulled her toward him so fiercely that there was not an inch of space between them. He kissed her with such passion that she thought she might die from a want of air in her lungs. His hands roamed over her back, creating a riot of sensations in places that had never felt a man's touch. She ignored the uneasy fluttering in her stomach. Her mind was decided.

Then just as suddenly, William thrust her away from him. "No, no." He kept her at arms' length, both hands on her shoulders as he stared down at the ground. "This is not right."

She took his hands and clasped them in front of her. "William, I can never be your bride or any man's. Let us at least have today."

His eyes, gaunt with need, shot up to her face and stared at her searchingly. He slowly shook his head. "No…I do not believe…no. I cannot take that from you."

"Then we will have nothing." Her voice was flat.

"We will find a way," he insisted. "I will marry you yet, Elizabeth Bennet."

"I do not have your faith," Elizabeth said quietly as she pulled up her sleeve until her shoulder was properly covered. "And every day risks discovery. I think it best if I vacate this place. This house."

His face was anguished. "No…"

She swallowed, forcing herself to voice what she preferred to leave unsaid. "This is too difficult, being here and knowing I cannot be yours. I will leave tomorrow."

"Where will you go?" he asked, his voice cracking on the last word.

"I do not know." Her eyes burned. "Perhaps I will leave London. I may not be suited to living in such a big city."

He clenched her hands tightly. "Do not leave tomorrow. At least come to dinner at Darcy House tomorrow night."

"To say goodbye?"

He swallowed. "If you wish."

She sighed. It was difficult to deny him anything. "Very well. Tomorrow night, but I will depart the day after."

***

Elizabeth closed her trunk and fixed the latch. Her few remaining belongings would fit into a small valise. Lately all she seemed to do was pack and unpack. After years of staying in Hertfordshire and longing to travel, now she never seemed to stay in one place for very long. But being a traveler was not nearly as entertaining as she had anticipated. *Be careful what you wish for.*

After tonight's dinner at Darcy House, she would spend one last night in the cottage with Emily and then depart for…she knew not where. Elizabeth had the vague idea that it would be nice to see the ocean, so perhaps a seaside town. But such places were often dear; she might do better to live somewhere less expensive. Of course, the best place to live would be where she might find employment, although Elizabeth did not know where that might be. However, she was determined to leave London; proximity to Mr. Darcy was simply too tempting.

Her eyes were wet again; Elizabeth wiped them impatiently. She had said goodbye to Longbourn, perhaps forever. Why should leaving this cottage—where she had spent only a handful of days—be more fraught with emotion? Actually it was better not to dwell on the reason. There was no point.

She sank heavily onto the bed, staring at the trunk. Her motto had always been "think only of the past as its remembrance gives you pleasure," yet it was difficult not to consider what might have happened if Lord Henry had not taken a liking to her. Perhaps then Mr. Darcy might have courted her properly, and they could be married.

She smiled at her own foolishness. Her life might have changed in many different ways. Lord Henry's actions had brought Mr. Darcy to Hertfordshire for the second time. Absent the attack at Lucas Lodge, she might never have seen Mr. Darcy again—and she would never have known he harbored a secret passion for her. She would have continued to believe he was a proud and difficult man.

That would have been for the best, surely.

She bit her lip, considering. Would she have given up the few moments of stolen kisses and whispered endearments to save herself from the ensuing heartbreak?

His passion for her was like a strong wine. It made her giddy with excitement. And they had created some beautiful memories which she could stow in the secret recesses of her heart and take out to warm herself on cold, lonely nights. No, she was pleased she had known that passion, even though she must surrender it so quickly.

But it would be so simple to stay at the cottage and enjoy Mr. Darcy's company. She could easily envision it. He would visit regularly, and they would share interesting conversation…and kisses. She would be safe here, without any need to find employment…

Elizabeth stiffened. *It would tantamount to becoming Will—Mr. Darcy's mistress.* No, she could never compromise herself that way. It would bring more shame on her family, and she would have not only lost her reputation but also her honor. Every day she would know she had compromised her values. Elizabeth brought a hand to her lips as if she could feel remembered kisses. That path had already beckoned to her. The sooner she left the cottage, the better.

I will not dwell on what might have been. I am not formed for sorrow. She dashed away a tear that trickled down her cheek. Once she was gone from London, her impossible obsession with Mr. Darcy would fade, surely.

Yes. She merely needed to wait for that.

***

Darcy regarded himself in the mirror. Perhaps he should have chosen the green waistcoat. But he had already changed his mind three times, and it was driving Perkins, his valet, to distraction. At least his cravat was well tied, but his hair… Darcy fussed with it. Must it hang over his forehead in such a way?

A sigh emanated from the other side of the room. Perkins was not above editorializing when he thought his master's behavior was excessive. Darcy let his hand drop. He wanted to look his best for dinner with Elizabeth tonight, but in actuality, his appearance would hardly matter. After she had decided to leave the cottage and Darcy, did he really believe a well-tied cravat would change her mind? She might avoid looking at him altogether since it was his presence that was chasing her from London. At least she was willing to break bread with him. All day he lived in fear of receiving a note announcing her "sudden indisposition."

During a sleepless night, he had berated himself for his untoward behavior. Elizabeth had been treated callously by the viscount, but Darcy's behavior had been little better. Yes, she had desired a few kisses, but Darcy had pushed for more—and had talked of marriage again when he knew it made her uneasy. Why had he been so impatient? That had been the moment when she decided she must flee not only Darcy himself but all of London.

At least there was hope she would remember him more fondly than Lord Henry.

Of course, that was a particularly low standard to meet.

The dinner should last about two hours. So he had that time to somehow find an argument that would convince Elizabeth to stay. He would vow never to visit the cottage or burden her with his presence. Perhaps if he promised that, she would at least agree to maintain a friendship with Georgiana, who would tell Darcy how she fared.

He had obsessed over the details of the menu with the cook and considered where to place Elizabeth at the dinner table, as if the right combination of dishes and seating could somehow induce her to remain. Instead, he should have been preparing words to convince her to stay.

If only he had his cousin's easy amiability. Richard would know how to apologize to a woman and persuade her to stay.

Darcy frowned at his reflection. It was very likely he would make a complete hash of the entire affair. Blast and damnation!

At the sound of a knock on the front door, Darcy's insides turned to ice. She was here. He had only the span of a dinner to persuade her to stay.

***

Darcy had wanted Elizabeth's last dinner at Darcy House to be a joyous affair, full of the witty banter and laughter she had brought into the Darcys' lives. Perhaps a reminder of good times would convince her to stay—and he might be able to mention some reasons for her to remain. Failing that, he was completely prepared to beg and plead at the end of the meal.

However, the meal had not gone as he hoped. He laughed at her jibes and listened eagerly to her opinions about *Henry V*, but he had failed to find a way to raise the subject of her departure.

An occasional pensive look from Georgiana suggested that she was also distressed at their imminent separation. Their guest seemed in high spirits, but perhaps her happiness was a bit forced. When the footman cleared the plates for the second course, Elizabeth's was still full of food.

At least he could eagerly anticipate the end of the meal when Elizabeth and Georgiana would perform their duet. Music always served to distract him.

Distraction came sooner than that, but not in the form he would have liked.

They had not yet reached the sweets course when Edwards, the butler, entered and announced, "Lady Catherine de Bourgh has arrived, sir."

Chapter Fifteen

To say that those words were unwelcome would be a vast understatement. Georgiana gasped, and Elizabeth turned pale. Darcy rose from his chair, casting about the room for a place to conceal their guest, but there was only one door, and the curtains were made of lace.

Before he could so much as utter a word to Elizabeth about the impending disaster, his aunt was upon them. Lady Catherine de Bourgh marched into the room as if it were hers to command. Anne de Bourgh and her companion trailed in her wake. And then—much to Darcy's horror—Mr. Collins scuttled into the room behind them. *Aunt Catherine must think herself very grand, traveling with her personal clergyman at her side.*

"Aunt Catherine!" Darcy gave her a slight bow, which she acknowledged with a regal nod of her head. "This is quite a surprise. I thought you still in Kent."

She drew herself up to her full height. "Kent is quite dull this time of year. I thought Town might provide more amusement, and there is a doctor here who might help Anne."

Darcy had no choice about how to proceed. "W-will you join us for dinner? We just finished the second remove."

His aunt regarded the elegant dining table as if it were covered with garbage. "Very well." Her tone suggested that she was granting him a favor. Footmen hurried to set places for four more guests, and Darcy worried fleetingly if his kitchen had sufficient food. But there were greater concerns; Collins was staring open-mouthed at his cousin, who was doing her best to look innocuous.

Well, there was nothing for it. He gestured to Elizabeth. "Lady Catherine, allow me to present Elizabeth Bennet of Longbourn House in Hertfordshire." Elizabeth stood and curtsied.

Aunt Catherine scanned Elizabeth from head to toe with her most disdainful look, but she did not sneer. From this, Darcy concluded that his aunt knew Elizabeth's identity but had not heard the vicious rumors about her reputation. Collins, standing behind his patroness, watched with wide eyes, his hand over his mouth, as if witnessing a terrible carriage accident. No doubt he was debating whether he should extract his Lady Catherine from the den of iniquity at once.

Darcy had no sympathy for the man.

Darcy immediately invited them all to sit, making it that much more awkward for Collins to insist on a departure. As the new arrivals were served by the footmen, the initial conversation was limited to the weather and the food. Collins fidgeted in his chair and glanced at Elizabeth several times a minute as if hoping she would somehow evaporate into thin air.

Elizabeth participated little in the conversation, but she did her best to act as if she belonged at Darcy House.

Finally, Collins could hold back his curiosity no longer. "Cousin, how do you happen to be at Darcy House?"

Darcy had been preparing an answer to this question. "I happened to encounter Miss Bennet here in London and invited her to dinner." This was all true, even if he was omitting details about *how* he had encountered Elizabeth and *when* she had been invited to dinner.

"I see." Collins practically quivered with indignation but dared not criticize Lady Catherine's nephew. There was a pause as Collins cut his meat. Then he gave Elizabeth a sidelong glance. "I hope you found the pamphlets I gave you to be instructive."

Darcy barely refrained from rolling his eyes; he could only imagine what kind of pamphlets Collins would bestow on a "fallen woman."

Elizabeth's eyes danced with amusement. "Indeed, they were quite full of instructions."

Beside Darcy, Georgiana smothered a giggle.

Collins frowned at his meat as if he could not figure out exactly where the conversation had gone astray. "Fortunately, I have brought additional pamphlets you might find edifying. One always encounters sinners in London."

"Indeed, sinners are everywhere," Elizabeth remarked dryly. "Perhaps in this very house."

Collins's eyes darted around the room as if they were about to be set upon by ruffians. Georgiana was again laughing into her napkin. Darcy almost felt sorry for the man; in a battle of wits with Elizabeth, Collins was unarmed.

"Is Charlotte in good health?" Elizabeth asked him.

"Yes, quite the picture of health!" Collins exclaimed. "We keep hoping for a certain blessed event, but alas it has not been forthcoming. I have been very diligent in performing my marital duties, however, so I am sure it will be but a short time."

Darcy had no desire to picture Collins performing his "marital duties." From the sour look on his aunt's face, she shared the sentiment. Georgiana's face, on the other hand, was red with suppressed laughter.

He was about to introduce a new subject to the discourse when his aunt directed a question to Elizabeth. "Are you the Miss Bennet who had the encounter with Viscount Billington?" she drawled before taking a sip of wine.

Collins nearly choked on the meat he was chewing. "How did you— that is, I did not know your ladyship was aware of that…er…incident."

Aunt Catherine regarded her vicar coolly over the rim of her wine glass. "*Mrs. Collins* informed me of it."

"When?" Panic edged his voice. "That is—I was not present when—"

"I do not invite you to every social gathering," Lady Catherine said imperiously. "Upon occasion, I prefer a gathering to include only women."

Collins's eyes bulged. "N-naturally, your ladyship," he spluttered.

Aunt Catherine turned away from Collins, dismissing him. "Well, answer me, girl," she demanded of Elizabeth.

Darcy felt ill. This was the very worst possible outcome for the dinner. He had brought Elizabeth here, trying to improve her life and hoping to convince her to stay. Now his relatives would make her feel like a pariah again. *She will rush to take the first mail coach out of London in the morning. It is an utter disaster, and I can do nothing to prevent it.*

Elizabeth lifted her chin, but the hand holding her fork was trembling. "I am."

"Good." Aunt Catherine gave a sharp nod. "I had been planning to pay you a call, but now you save me a ride to Hertfordshire."

Elizabeth looked as perplexed as Darcy felt. Would his aunt really have traveled all the way to Hertfordshire to personally condemn the behavior of a woman she had never met? "Pay me a call?" Elizabeth asked.

"Yes." Her tone was as sharp and imperious as always. "I wished to offer you my sympathy for the way you were treated by Lord Henry."

Darcy suddenly felt lightheaded and was grateful to be seated. Georgiana choked on her wine and coughed loudly.

Elizabeth's eyes were as wide as saucers. "Y-your l-ladyship is acquainted with Lord Henry?" Elizabeth asked.

Aunt Catherine gave a most unladylike snort. "I certainly am. He attempted a similar scheme with Anne." She gestured to her daughter, who nodded meekly. "Enticed her into a library during a ball with the aim of compromising her and getting his hands on the de Bourgh fortune. Fortunately, I keep a close watch on Anne and foiled his plan."

"Oh, how horrible!" Georgiana gasped.

"I do not know why he would bother to compromise you." Aunt Catherine flicked a hand in Elizabeth's direction. "I understand you have no fortune to speak of, although I suppose you are moderately pretty."

Elizabeth pursed her lips. Was she attempting to hold back a laugh? "One never knows," she said solemnly.

"Then there was a parson's daughter in Kent," Aunt Catherine proclaimed. "Billington ruined her reputation, and she had no choice but to become his mistress. He bought her a little cottage but then abandoned her a few months later. Occasionally I have a footman take her some fruit or meat—when I think of it."

"You are the soul of generosity, ma'am," Collins intoned.

Her ladyship took another sip of wine, enjoying the audience. "It is disgraceful the way Lord Henry treated her! And apparently she is not the only one he has used in such a way. He makes it something of a practice to ruin respectable young ladies and force them into unseemly relationships."

Still reeling from his aunt's unexpected sympathy, Darcy could only manage to say, "Indeed." Thank Providence that had not been Elizabeth's fate!

"Someone should prevent such wanton behavior!" Aunt Catherine shook her head sadly. Darcy felt a surge of anger; his aunt had known of the man's behavior but could not bestir herself to do anything about it. "Really, he deserves a reckoning. He should be stopped."

"Indeed." Elizabeth laid her napkin on the table. "And I believe I know how."

***

Elizabeth knocked on the rough-hewn wooden door, hoping her quarry was at home. Mr. Darcy had not wanted her to visit the cottage alone, but Elizabeth had insisted. The other woman might be reluctant to speak in the company of a man.

She was about to knock again when the door opened to reveal a pretty, plainly dressed woman. "Sarah Newsome?" Elizabeth asked.

The woman flinched at the sound of her name. "What do you want?"

"I just want to talk. I was given your name by Lady Catherine at Rosings Park."

Sarah's body lost some of its tension. "Talk about what?" she asked.

"Lord Henry Carson." Sarah flinched again. Elizabeth hurried through the rest of her speech before the woman shut the door in her face. "I know that he has behaved in a most ungentlemanly fashion toward you—and other women. I do not believe the viscount's behavior should continue unchecked. I hope you can help me put an end to it."

Sarah rolled her eyes. "Aye, but how do you stop him? He's a lord!"

Elizabeth grimaced. She had heard that sentiment many times in the past week. "I have a plan, but I need information from you. I understand you had an encounter with him that ended unpleasantly?"

Sarah laughed bitterly. "Aye, to put it delicately."

Elizabeth bit her lip. She hated asking a stranger to discuss something so personal. "He wanted to force me into becoming his mistress. Is that what happened to you?"

Sarah gave her a level look. "He forced me all right. But I didn't become his mistress." She sighed and backed away from the doorway. Behind her, a little boy of about three years toddled into view.

Elizabeth could not prevent the widening of her eyes. Clearly she had not heard the whole story.

Sarah looked over her shoulder at the boy and smiled fondly. Then she turned back to Elizabeth with a sigh. "You may as well come in. It's a long story."

Chapter Sixteen

Elizabeth awoke to the sight of her familiar childhood canopy bed. She had only been back at Longbourn one night, but already she missed the little cottage in London. It was not nearly as grand as Longbourn, but it had been comfortable, and it had been hers—and she had enjoyed an unprecedented amount of privacy there.

At least in the privacy of her own head, Elizabeth could be perfectly honest: she also missed dining at Darcy House, and Georgiana, and…most of all, Mr. Darcy. She had grown accustomed to the freedoms her cottage had afforded them. The long conversations…the kisses…the caresses. Despite the temptation to go further than was prudent, those weeks had been a magical time for her. *I hope the plan works.* If Elizabeth could not wring the truth from Lord Henry, she would need to surrender the cottage and Mr. Darcy—in favor of a solitary life somewhere far away from London.

Blinking, she tried to keep tears at bay. If the worst happened, the temptation to become Mr. Darcy's mistress would be great. Elizabeth was shocked that she could even think such a thing, but it was true. She was in love with the man, and already an absence of two days depressed her spirits. However, if her plan did not work, she could not wed Mr. Darcy. It would destroy his life and his sister's. And she loved them both too much to be the instrument of their destruction.

He would arrive in Hertfordshire today, and her eyes were hungry for the sight of him. But they would see each other only in public, with the gazes of many other people upon them. They would not enjoy any time alone.

Elizabeth threw back the covers and stood. It was time to face the day. Jane had arisen earlier, so Elizabeth had the room to herself as she removed her nightrail and donned a chemise. It had taken nearly a month to bring the pieces of the plan together. When they had first devised the scheme, Elizabeth had been very hopeful, but now doubts swarmed her.

She pulled on her dress, a plain one that buttoned down the front. Mr. Darcy had emphasized how she must appear to be sad and downtrodden—defeated by the necessity of returning to Longbourn. Hopefully word of her demeanor would reach Lord Henry, and he would not be suspicious despite Mr. Darcy's presence.

Tonight would decide the success of their plan—whether they would reveal the viscount for who he really was. If the plan failed, it would further blacken Elizabeth's name, although it could hardly make her situation worse. Still, Lord Henry seemed to hold all the cards, not the least of which was everyone's tendency to believe a titled gentleman's words above all others. On the other hand, their plan depended on everything working perfectly, plus a little bit of good luck. They had tried to leave as little as possible to chance, but she could imagine any number of things that could go wrong.

Mr. Darcy thought it a very good plan, but Elizabeth believed he was only trying to brighten her spirits. In truth, she believed the odds of its success were low and was reluctant to place too much hope in a future that might never occur.

She sat on the edge of the bed to draw on her stockings. She would have to see the plan through. It was her only hope of vindication, and Mr. Darcy was counting on it. Elizabeth sighed. He would be terribly disappointed if it did not work. He had woven a nice fantasy of a future together.

She slipped on her shoes and buckled them as she thought through the different parts of the plan. One crucial element was Mr. Bingley. He had arrived at Netherfield last week. Despite her doubts and worries, Elizabeth smiled at the thought of how Mr. Bingley and Jane had been enjoying long walks through the neighborhood. If all else failed, hopefully something good would come of their reunion.

When Elizabeth found that Mr. Darcy and Miss Bingley believed Jane to be indifferent to Mr. Bingley's affections, she had persuaded Mr. Darcy otherwise. He informed his friend of this new information, whereupon Mr. Bingley declared his immediate desire to return to Meryton. Miss Bingley had wailed about the scandal attached to the Bennet family, but Mr. Bingley had been determined. In fact, it was all Mr. Darcy could do to get his friend to delay returning to Hertfordshire until their plan was in place.

Immediately upon returning to Netherfield, Mr. Bingley issued an invitation to a ball. Lord Henry, naturally, had received an invitation—as had the Bennet family, much to the disgust of some town gossips. The ball was tonight. By midnight they would know Elizabeth's fate.

A rattling sound came from the window. What could that be? It came again as if something hard was glancing off the window panes. Elizabeth hurried over and drew back the curtains.

Below her window, partially hidden behind a pine tree, stood Mr. Darcy—ready with another handful of gravel to throw at her window. When he saw her face, he smiled and beckoned her down.

Elizabeth shook her head fondly as she hurried out of the room. He was not supposed to be in Meryton already, and he should not have taken the foolish risk to be on her family's property. At the same time, she was inordinately pleased to see him.

Elizabeth rushed down the stairs, pausing only to grab a shawl before she scrambled through the back door. Mr. Darcy was not immediately visible, but Elizabeth ran around the back of the pine tree that she had seen out of the window. Sure enough, there he stood, shielded from any eyes in the house. *I should greet him properly with a staid curtesy and an inquiry after his family's health.*

But she ran into his arms and received a passionate kiss which seemed to go on forever—and yet it was far too brief.

The need for breath finally forced their lips apart, but Mr. Darcy would not release Elizabeth. He held her against his chest as his lips caressed her ear. "My love! It has been far too long."

She wanted to tease him that it had only been two days, but she felt the same way.

"I did not expect you so soon," she said.

"I hoped if I arrived early that I could steal a few moments with you." She squeezed him in her arms to show her appreciation. "Everything is in readiness," he said. "Aunt Catherine will arrive today with her charges."

She nodded, although her body must have stiffened, for Mr. Darcy pulled back and regarded her searchingly. "Are you having doubts about the plan?"

If only he were not so good at reading her every emotion! "It is a good plan, the best plan we could devise under the circumstances. But it does rely heavily on the good judgment of others."

He shrugged. "We had no choice in that regard."

"I no longer have much faith in others' good judgment, I am afraid," she admitted.

"I understand," he said gently as he ran his fingertips along her cheek, causing shivers up and down her spine. "But it will work." His voice was low but firm and full of conviction.

She nodded, wishing she had his faith.

He clasped both of her hands between his and squeezed. "We *will* clear your name."

As he leaned forward, his lips captured hers. Elizabeth enjoyed the kiss, but part of her mind could not help planning what she would do if everything went awry.

***

It had taken a great deal of maneuvering to have Lord Pippinworth in the Netherfield library. Lord Pippinworth Grassley, Earl of Minington, was well known as an authority on moral matters. The author of the well-known *Gentleman's Guide to Being a Gentleman*, he was frequently quoted in good company. Darcy rather suspected that few people had actually read the *Gentleman's Guide*; they were only familiar enough with the quotations to appear suitably conversant with the text. Darcy once considered reading it but discovered it to be the most dull, didactic tome he had ever encountered.

But Lord Pippinworth himself enjoyed an unsurpassed reputation. He had been quite devoted to his wife, who passed away a few years ago. His children were known for being moral exemplars. His reputation for being fair and impartial meant that he was often sought to arbitrate disputes or resolve difficult questions of etiquette. A big bear of a man with a thick head of black hair and a bushy, very unfashionable mustache, Lord Pippinworth was *the* authority on morality.

So when Darcy learned that Pippinworth was in Hertfordshire, a mere half an hour's drive from Netherfield, he begged Bingley to invite the man. Although somewhat mystified, Bingley had gladly acquiesced.

From Pippinworth's entry into Netherfield, Darcy had been his constant companion, ensuring that the man had drink and food and lively conversation. Ultimately he had persuaded the man to accompany him to Netherfield's grand but sparsely furnished library.

As they entered the library, Darcy left off the pleasantries in favor of explaining the business at hand. "Lord Pippinworth, there is actually a matter that I would particularly like your assistance with," he explained as they took seats in the otherwise unpopulated room.

"Oh?" The other man smoothed his mustache, flattered and pleased.

"In your book, you emphasize how a gentleman must always take responsibility for his actions." This was so glaringly obvious to Darcy that he thought it a pity it needed to be written down at all.

"Yes, chapter two." The lord smiled.

Darcy fervently hoped the man would not ask pointed questions about the text since he was only conversant with those parts that were frequently discussed in society. "Exactly. But I have a friend—well, an acquaintance—who is refusing to take responsibility for his actions. And as a result, a woman's reputation is suffering."

"How shocking!" the lord exclaimed. "Why this is terrible behavior!"

"Indeed. I was hoping for your assistance in persuading him back to the proper course of action." Darcy regarded the other man soberly. Pippinworth was friendly with Lord Henry and would no doubt be appalled when he learned of the viscount's behavior.

Lord Pippinworth straightened his spine. "I will certainly try. It is my opinion that some men are naturally of a bad nature, but only very few. Most can be persuaded to see the error of their ways. My own nephew, Thomas Cherborg, had an unusual fondness for drink. I sat the young man down and explained to him all of the evils that could befall a man from excessive imbibing. Afterward he thanked me; he said the scales had fallen from his eyes."

Darcy smiled and nodded politely. "And he ceased drinking?"

The lord shifted in his seat. "Well, er, not altogether. But I do believe he reduced the quantity, particularly after that incident where he fell down the stairs."

Darcy nodded solemnly. "I see. How fortunate you spoke with him."

"Many men do need strong moral guidance." Pippinworth settled back into his chair. "Now, consider the situation of Bradley Crawford—"

Fortunately, Darcy was spared another morally edifying tale by the arrival of Bingley—with Lord Henry in tow.

"Pippinworth wanted to see me?" the viscount exclaimed with some alarm as they strolled through the doorway. Darcy scarcely blamed him. Moral disapprobation as potent as Pippinworth's was something to be feared.

"Bingley, Billington." Lord Pippinworth nodded to the newcomers.

"Actually, *I* asked Bingley to bring you here," Darcy admitted to Lord Henry. The viscount's eyes narrowed, and his lip curled as he regarded Darcy. "There is a matter which must be resolved, a matter that concerns a lady's honor."

Lord Henry crossed his arms over his chest defiantly. There was no doubt he knew which lady Darcy meant. "I cannot imagine which matter you refer to."

"Miss Elizabeth Bennet," Darcy said. "You were found alone in a drawing room with her some three months ago, ruining her reputation."

The viscount smirked. Darcy would have liked to remove that grin with his fist. "I did attempt to make amends for that unfortunate situation," Lord Henry said smoothly. "I offered her my hand, but she declined."

"Which is, in fact, her prerogative." Darcy turned to Lord Pippinworth. "Would you not agree, sir? If the woman in question does not care for the man, she should not be forced to wed him?"

The lord cleared his throat. "Well, of course not, but marriage is always the best choice. She would be well-advised to accept him."

"But she has not."

"As we have established," Lord Henry spoke quickly. "There is nothing we can resolve here. I do not see a purpose in this exercise." He turned toward the door.

"But there is the matter of the babe," Darcy said. "You should still take responsibility for your own get." Bingley gasped and turned white.

The viscount froze in his tracks and then spun around, stalking toward Darcy with his finger outstretched. "I did not get her with child!" he cried. "It is none of mine. You cannot pin a child on me! I kissed her, nothing more!"

Darcy leaned back against the library table and smiled. "In fact, Miss Elizabeth is *not* with child." He paused a moment to allow everyone to understand the implications. "If you only stole a few kisses, sir, why did you allow the other guests—all of Meryton, in fact— to believe you had taken her virtue?"

Lord Henry spluttered, turning red in the face.

Lord Pippinworth marched toward the other man. "Yes, that is an interesting question. Why did you tell falsehoods that ruined the woman's reputation? You know it is our duty as gentlemen to safeguard women's virtue."

"I-I—"

Darcy had no intention of letting the viscount speak just yet. "Was it perhaps because she had spurned your advances, and you thought you could force her into your bed?"

"No—I—"

"Is that true, Henry?" Lord Pippinworth asked. "Why, that would be terrible! I thought better of you. I never believed you would stoop to such devices."

"It is a lie!" Little drops of spittle flew from the viscount's mouth. "I have no trouble finding a woman to warm my bed if I wish!"

"How delightful," Lord Pippinworth said disdainfully.

"Perhaps not," Darcy admitted. "But you would prefer to force them, would you not? You prefer a woman who cannot tell you no."

"Really, Henry, that is most ungentlemanly of you," murmured Lord Pippinworth.

"That is not true!" Lord Henry cried. "I may have been…overly zealous with Elizabeth Bennet, but it is certainly not my habit to force women into an untenable position. I would never—"

Darcy interrupted. "Let us ascertain the truth of the matter, shall we?" He gestured to Bingley. "I pray you, open the door."

Somewhat bemused, Bingley strode to the door and opened it.

Darcy called out, "Miss Elizabeth, you may enter, and please bring your friends."

Darcy would admit to being biased, but Elizabeth looked particularly beautiful that evening. She wore a cream-colored satin gown, ornamented with small pink rosettes. Georgiana had lent her a matching headband that looked a bit like a tiara. The effect was magnificent.

Three women trailed behind her, not as richly dressed, but no doubt they were wearing their best gowns. Lady Catherine de Bourgh followed this procession, regarding Lord Henry as she might a strange insect, with Anne de Bourgh and her companion trailing in her ladyship's wake. A small crowd of onlookers followed, no doubt curious about the nature of the activities in the library, a room which customarily did not see much traffic during a ball. They crowded around the library doorway, watching curiously.

Lord Henry had been belligerent at the sight of Elizabeth, but the color drained from his face as the three women—all glaring at him defiantly—filed in. He barely registered Lady Catherine's presence.

"Who are these women?" Lord Pippinworth asked in a booming voice.

Elizabeth gave the lord a quick curtsey. "I am Elizabeth Bennet. May I present my friends: Sarah Carson, Mary Carson, and Gwendolyn Carson."

Lord Pippinworth frowned. "Carson?" He glanced at Lord Henry. "I was not aware you had any sisters."

"He does not," Elizabeth intoned. "In fact, these women are his wives."

Chapter Seventeen

"What? All of them?" Lord Pippinworth cried, his voice nearly drowned out by the surprised exclamations from the crowd.

"Don't be ridiculous!" Lord Henry cried. "This is a misunderstanding. I would never—"

"As you say, your lordship," Elizabeth addressed Lord Pippinworth as if the viscount had not spoken. The three women nodded their agreement. "Sarah is a minister's daughter whom Lord Henry compromised in Kent; he offered her marriage four years ago to make amends. Coincidentally, Mary found herself in much the same situation three years ago in Sussex. He married her but lived with her only a few months before disappearing. Gwendolyn was a shop girl whom Lord Henry married most recently." All three women stared implacably at the viscount.

Lord Henry scoffed. "I have no idea what Miss Bennet is about. I admit I know these women, but I did not marry them. This woman and Darcy have some kind of vendetta against me—they seek to ruin my good name."

People in the little crowd were looking at each other, wondering if he could be right. Many of the onlookers regarded Lord Henry sympathetically. Damn, the man could be persuasive. How would they counter this? The women could testify, but that would pit their words against the viscount's. And their story was a fantastical one. They had made so much progress; could it all fall apart now? He gave Elizabeth a despairing look, but her eyes were on...Anne de Bourgh?

Anne stepped forward, holding up a few pieces of paper, and spoke in a surprisingly clear voice. "I have in my possession letters from clergymen at three parish churches confirming that Lord Henry's three marriages are all recorded in their church's registries. Apparently his lordship bribed the right people so that his duplicity would not be discovered." This began another round of exclamations among the onlookers; now expressions directed at Lord Henry were decidedly less friendly.

"Thank you, Miss de Bourgh." Elizabeth smiled at Anne, who returned to her thunderstruck mother.

"Furthermore," Elizabeth continued, glaring directly at the viscount, "you made *me* an offer of marriage, which I must decline—again. I believe you have a surfeit of wives as it is."

Lord Pippinworth took a step forward, his eyes darting from the women to Lord Henry and back again. "This-this is quite shocking! Henry, how could you—?"

"I support all the women!" Lord Henry cried. "They want for nothing. They have not been ill-treated."

Elizabeth snorted. "They have been compromised, lied to, and taken advantage of. You have ruined their lives!"

Darcy stepped in. "And you attempted to do the same to Miss Bennet. But she confounded your scheme by refusing your offer of marriage." The small crowd in the doorway nodded in agreement, murmuring about Elizabeth's wisdom in refusing the viscount.

Lord Pippinworth cleared his throat. "Then there is the matter of bigamy. You do know bigamy is against the law, Henry? They might allow it in some Far Eastern countries, but it is illegal in England!"

Lord Henry stared at Lord Pippinworth in horror for a long moment. Without warning, he turned and raced for the door. But the doorway was now so crowded with curious onlookers that many bodies blocked his way. Lord Henry was manhandled back into the library and pushed into a chair.

Lord Pippinworth loomed over him. "I shall send for the magistrate. This is a very serious matter." Lord Henry shrank down in the chair and said nothing.

Darcy cleared his throat. "Perhaps we should bind him until the magistrate arrives. We would not want him to make another attempt at escape."

"An excellent idea," Lord Pippinworth boomed and immediately sent a young man to the stable for some rope. He then approached the three Mrs. Carsons. "I apologize for the behavior of this reprobate, ladies. I will personally ensure that you obtain the divorces you require and that you will be provided for."

"Thank you, sir," Sarah Carson responded. The other women nodded appreciatively.

"And Miss Bennet." The man turned to Elizabeth. "You are to be commended for having the greatness of mind to recognize this snake for what he is." Elizabeth merely nodded her thanks.

The gathering had dissolved into many small knots of people discussing this shocking turn of events in the most animated tones. Lady Mary, the viscount's aunt, emerged from the crowd and approached Elizabeth. "I owe you the deepest apologies, Miss Elizabeth, for not believing your account of the events in the drawing room." She cast a scathing look at Lord Henry. "It is now apparent that neither I nor anybody else should ever have believed a word my nephew told us." She took one of Elizabeth's hands and patted it comfortingly. "Will you forgive me?"

Elizabeth's cheeks were deeply flushed. "Of course, Lady Mary. All is forgiven and forgotten."

As Elizabeth continued to speak with Lady Mary, Darcy scanned the crowd for some Bennets but saw only Jane. If anyone owed Elizabeth an apology, it was her own family. Hopefully they would relay it in private.

Lady Mary was now looming over her still-bound nephew and castigating him for his perfidies. Lord Pippinworth took her place, clasping Elizabeth's hands in his. "Miss Bennet, I have ensured everyone is aware of Lord Henry's admission that he lied about compromising your virtue. Anyone who claims otherwise may answer to me!"

"Thank you, your lordship," Elizabeth said.

"It is the least I could do after you revealed his duplicity to the world! Three wives! Just imagine." He shook his head sadly. "You have done England quite a service today."

Elizabeth blushed even more deeply. "I had help. Miss de Bourgh provided valuable assistance."

The lord nodded approvingly. "Quite a clever girl."

"And Mr. Darcy facilitated much of this," Elizabeth continued.

Releasing Elizabeth's hand, Lord Pippinworth clapped Darcy on the back. "Well done, Darcy!"

Darcy shook his head. "I must give credit where credit is due. Miss Elizabeth did the hard work."

Lord Pippinworth looked from Darcy to Elizabeth and back, his eyes narrowed. Then he chuckled knowingly at Darcy. "Yes, indeed, it is important to give credit where it is due. That is the way to woo her!"

Darcy knew he was blushing as the lord walked away laughing.

***

Mr. Darcy and the lord recruited a couple of sturdy men to strong-arm the viscount out of the library and into the kitchen to await the pleasure of the magistrate. Elizabeth watched him go with a tremendous sense of relief; the man and his lies had ruled her life for months. Now the fight was over. Lord Henry's perfidy had been made public. Elizabeth's name had been cleared before enough witnesses that there would never be a doubt about her virtue.

She felt lighter than she had in a long time but also a little unmoored. What should she do now? The last few months of her life had been entirely directed by Lord Henry and his actions. Now she was free to resume the life she had led before his interference. There was nothing to bar her from returning to Longbourn, and she would certainly be pleased to spend time with Jane and her father. Her mother and other sisters, however, were a different matter. She did not blame them for believing the viscount's lies; it was in the nature of their characters. But she was hurt by their lack of faith in both her morality and her honesty, and she was not eager to share a roof with them.

Members of her family were interspersed throughout the crowd. Lydia and Kitty appeared bemused by the entire event and were loudly asking questions of anyone who would listen. Her mother declared that she knew about Elizabeth's innocence all along. Her father and Jane were far less vocal but were wreathed with smiles as they spoke to people about Elizabeth's vindication.

In fact, all around Elizabeth people talked with great animation about the stunning events of the ball. They laughed, drank punch, and milled about. Elizabeth stood, solitary and silent and unmoving—wondering what would become of her. Mr. Darcy certainly had mentioned plans for their future, but what if he had changed his mind? What if he had been thoroughly disgusted with the Bennets once again and wanted nothing to do with her? She could hardly blame him. Or what if he realized he had not felt love for her so much as pity?

Lord Pippinworth and Mr. Darcy had returned to the library and were talking like old friends by the time they reached Elizabeth. "The magistrate will need to speak with me; would you be so kind as to accompany us?" the lord asked Mr. Darcy. "You could give a full accounting of everything you have learned."

"I can visit him tomorrow," Mr. Darcy replied. "But I have more pressing business tonight." His eyes were on Elizabeth. *Why is he watching me?*

"At this time of night?" Lord Pippinworth exclaimed.

"It is extremely urgent," Mr. Darcy assured the other man.

The lord's eyes followed Mr. Darcy's and then widened. "Oh! Very good. I see." Lord Pippinworth gave Elizabeth a benevolent smile.

I wish he would explain it to me, Elizabeth thought. It was as if the two men were speaking in code.

Mr. Darcy took two steps toward her. With one eyebrow raised, he had an expectant look in his eye, but Elizabeth was entirely mystified. His eyes caught and held hers; she could look nowhere else.

Then he got down on one knee. There were gasps from the assembled onlookers. All conversation ceased, and all eyes were on them.

"Miss Bennet, now that your name has been cleared, I am hoping there are no other objections to our union. I esteem you. I admire you. I love you. I beg you to be my wife." His expression was somber.

Does he fear I will refuse him again?

Was that why he has made this proposal in public?

She could not let him dwell in an agony of ignorance for one more moment. "Mr. Darcy, I would be honored to be your wife."

Mr. Darcy's smile was blinding as he instantly sprang to his feet, enveloping her in his embrace. Elizabeth scarcely had time to draw breath before he kissed her. The onlookers gasped and giggled at this breach of decorum.

Her mother's voice floated above the hubbub. "Oh! Oh! Mr. Darcy! Who would have thought? Ten thousand a year. Who would have thought?"

Darcy's lips released hers, but he still held her, his mouth hovering near her ear. He huffed a little laugh at her mother's exclamations. "Yes, indeed, Elizabeth, who would have thought?" Then he kissed her again.

Epilogue

"Congratulations to Mr. and Mrs. Darcy!" Lady Catherine de Bourgh held her glass of champagne high, and the other guests of the wedding breakfast followed suit. Darcy took a sip of the champagne. Of course, it was a very good vintage; only the best would do at Rosings Park.

"I still cannot believe your aunt volunteered to host our wedding," Elizabeth murmured to him.

Darcy chuckled. "Nor can I."

Darcy and Anne had both informed Lady Catherine years ago that they had no intention of wedding, but she had still cherished the hope of a union. So she had been most put out when she learned her nephew had proposed in such a public fashion to an upstart country miss.

However, her fit of pique dissipated three days later when Anne de Bourgh announced her engagement to Lord Pippinworth. Following the events of the Netherfield ball, the lord and lady apparently had started a conversation which led them to agree to collaborate on the writing of *The Lady's Guide to Being a Lady*. Romance quickly blossomed. Apparently an earldom was an appropriate compensation for having lost her nephew as a bridegroom, and Aunt Catherine had immediately proposed that the cousins have a double wedding at Rosings Park. Lord and Lady Pippinworth were now holding court with their many admirers on the other side of the vast dining room.

Darcy had not been in favor of the idea initially, but Elizabeth had agreed—mostly for the sake of familial harmony. Having a wedding in Kent also had given Elizabeth an opportunity to live at Rosings for a month before the event. She had confessed to Darcy a desire to avoid returning to Longbourn. Although their engagement—and Lord Henry's confession of the truth— had gone a long way to repairing Elizabeth's reputation with both her family and the people of Meryton, she had not been eager to return home for any length of time.

Her mother and younger sisters had welcomed her back into the family as if they had never treated her like a pariah, but Elizabeth would need some time before she could be completely at ease with them. However, she had already made plans for Jane—and her new husband, Charles Bingley—to visit Pemberley after the wedding.

Sarah Carson approached, holding her toddling three-year-old boy by the hand. "Congratulations, Mr. and Mrs. Darcy! You deserve every happiness."

Elizabeth gave her a hug. "Thank you, Lady Sarah."

The woman blushed. "I am still unaccustomed to the title." She looked directly at Darcy. "And I would not have it if it were not for your efforts, sir. You have my most profound thanks."

Darcy shrugged. "It was the right thing to do."

Before charges could be brought against Lord Henry, he fled to the continent. Darcy rather suspected he had been allowed to escape by the magistrate, a friend of the viscount's aunt. The seriousness of his misdeeds, however, ensured that he would never again be able to return to England.

Lord Pippinworth and Darcy worked together to offer the man's erstwhile wives legal assistance in obtaining divorces. Gwendolyn and Mary had easily dissolved the marriage bonds since their unions had never been legitimate. As the first wife, Sarah Carson's situation was more difficult, but her petition for divorce was wending its way through the courts, and Darcy's lawyer was confident it would be granted.

However, when the dowager viscountess, Lord Henry's mother, had learned of Sarah's situation, she immediately extended an invitation for the young woman to live at Thornfield, the family's ancestral estate in Kent. The viscount had kept all three wives a secret from his family because he hoped to have a "legitimate" marriage with an heiress. Once Sarah was assured she need never fear facing Lord Henry on the premises, she gladly accepted the invitation. Apparently the two ladies got along very well. The circumstances were also beneficial for Sarah's son, Peter, who would one day inherit Thornfield and the title of viscount. Lady Sarah had pronounced herself very pleased with her situation.

Lady Sarah excused herself, taking her boy off to play, as Elizabeth's parents approached the newly married couple. Mrs. Bennet hugged her second oldest daughter. "Congratulations, Elizabeth! I must say it was very clever of you to turn down the viscount. Now you have this handsome husband and his ten thousand a year."

Elizabeth's face flushed, and she rolled her eyes. "Mama—"

Darcy nodded in agreement with his new mother-in-law. "Indeed, ma'am." Elizabeth's eyes widened at this declaration. "She was very clever to comprehend the viscount's true character when so many in Hertfordshire did not. So many people believed his lies, even about Elizabeth's true character."

Now it was Mrs. Bennet's turn to blush.

Darcy was not finished. "But I find Elizabeth's *courage* even more admirable. She had the strength of will to defy *all* the voices in Meryton and Longbourn who demanded she accede to the viscount's demands. And she had the courage to expose Lord Henry's crimes. Not only did she clear her own name, but she also freed three other women from their entanglements with the man."

"Y-yes, indeed!" Mrs. Bennet spluttered.

Elizabeth was still blushing, but now from his excessive praise.

Mr. Bennet was beaming, whether about his daughter's bravery or his wife's uncharacteristic speechlessness, Darcy did not know. Darcy turned to his new father-in-law. "You are to be commended on immediately seeing the truth of your daughter's story. You stood by her when nearly everyone had turned against her. For that reason alone, I shall always be grateful to you."

"I have never known Lizzy to lie," Mr. Bennet said stoutly. Mrs. Bennet appeared about to swoon.

"I hope you will come to visit Pemberley soon," Darcy continued. "I believe the library holds a number of books that would be of interest to you."

"I would like that very much," Mr. Bennet said.

After her parents wandered away, Elizabeth took her new husband's hand and squeezed it gently. "You, sir, are also to be commended for having faith in my innocence. You believed my story even before I told it to you."

"That is because I knew you, Elizabeth. I knew you would never behave the way the viscount would have everyone believe."

"You knew me better than my own family," she said in wonder. "Perhaps I should have realized sooner that it was a sign."

Darcy smiled at her. "A sign of what, my love?"

"That you are the right man for me."

"I am indeed," Darcy said and kissed her.

The End

Thank you for purchasing this book.

Your support makes it possible for authors like me to continue writing.

Please consider leaving a review where you purchased the book.

Learn more about me and my upcoming releases:

Sign up for my newsletter Dispatches from Pemberley

Website: www.victoriakincaid.com

Twitter: VictoriaKincaid@kincaidvic

Blog: https://kincaidvictoria.wordpress.com/

Facebook: https://www.facebook.com/kincaidvictoria

About Victoria Kincaid

The author of numerous best-selling Pride and Prejudice variations, historical romance writer Victoria Kincaid has a Ph.D. in English literature and runs a small business, er, household with two children, a hyperactive dog, an overly affectionate cat, and a husband who is not threatened by Mr. Darcy. They live near Washington DC, where the inhabitants occasionally stop talking about politics long enough to complain about the traffic.

On weekdays she is a freelance writer/editor who now specializes in IT marketing (it's more interesting than it sounds). In the past, some of her more…unusual writing subjects have included space toilets, taxi services, laser gynecology, bidets, orthopedic shoes, generating energy from onions, Ferrari rental car services, and vampire face lifts (she swears she is not making any of this up). A lifelong Austen fan, Victoria has read more Jane Austen variations and sequels than she can count – and confesses to an extreme partiality for the Colin Firth version of *Pride and Prejudice*.

Darcy vs. Bennet

Elizabeth Bennet is drawn to a handsome, mysterious man she meets at a masquerade ball. However, she gives up all hope for a future with him when she learns he is the son of George Darcy, the man who ruined her father's life. Despite her father's demand that she avoid the younger Darcy, when he appears in Hertfordshire Elizabeth cannot stop thinking about him, or seeking him out, or welcoming his kisses....

Fitzwilliam Darcy has struggled to carve out a life independent from his father's vindictive temperament and domineering ways, although the elder Darcy still controls the purse strings. After meeting Elizabeth Bennet, Darcy cannot imagine marrying anyone else, even though his father despises her family. More than anything he wants to make her his wife, but doing so would mean sacrificing everything else....

Mr. Darcy to the Rescue

When the irritating Mr. Collins proposes marriage, Elizabeth Bennet is prepared to refuse him, but then she learns that her father is ill. If Mr. Bennet dies, Collins will inherit Longbourn and her family will have nowhere to go. Elizabeth accepts the proposal, telling herself she can be content as long as her family is secure. If only she weren't dreading the approaching wedding day…

Ever since leaving Hertfordshire, Mr. Darcy has been trying to forget his inconvenient attraction to Elizabeth. News of her betrothal forces him to realize how devastating it would be to lose her. He arrives at Longbourn intending to prevent the marriage, but discovers Elizabeth's real opinion about his character. Then Darcy recognizes his true dilemma…

How can he rescue her when she doesn't want him to?

Chaos Comes to Longbourn

While attempting to suppress his desire to dance with Elizabeth Bennet, Mr. Darcy flees the Netherfield ballroom only to stumble upon a half-dressed Lydia Bennet in the library. When they are discovered in this compromising position by a shrieking Mrs. Bennet, it triggers a humorously improbable series of events. After the dust settles, eight of Jane Austen's characters are engaged to the wrong person.

Although Darcy yearns for Elizabeth, and she has developed feelings for the master of Pemberley, they are bound by promises to others. How can Darcy and Elizabeth unravel this tangle of hilariously misbegotten betrothals and reach their happily ever after?

Pride and Proposals

What if Mr. Darcy's proposal was too late?

Darcy has been bewitched by Elizabeth Bennet since he met her in Hertfordshire. He can no longer fight this overwhelming attraction and must admit he is hopelessly in love. During Elizabeth's visit to Kent she has been forced to endure the company of the difficult and disapproving Mr. Darcy, but she has enjoyed making the acquaintance of his affable cousin, Colonel Fitzwilliam.

Finally resolved, Darcy arrives at Hunsford Parsonage prepared to propose—only to discover that Elizabeth has just accepted a proposal from the Colonel, Darcy's dearest friend in the world. As he watches the couple prepare for a lifetime together, Darcy vows never to speak of what is in his heart. Elizabeth has reason to dislike Darcy, but finds that he haunts her thoughts and stirs her emotions in strange ways.

Can Darcy and Elizabeth find their happily ever after?

The Secrets of Darcy and Elizabeth

A despondent Darcy travels to Paris in the hopes of forgetting the disastrous proposal at Hunsford. Paris is teeming with English visitors during a brief moment of peace in the Napoleonic Wars, but Darcy's spirits don't lift until he attends a ball and unexpectedly encounters…Elizabeth Bennet! Darcy seizes the opportunity to correct misunderstandings and initiate a courtship.

Their moment of peace is interrupted by the news that England has again declared war on France, and hundreds of English travelers must flee Paris immediately. Circumstances force Darcy and Elizabeth to escape on their own, despite the risk to her reputation. Even as they face dangers from street gangs and French soldiers, romantic feelings blossom during their flight to the coast. But then Elizabeth falls ill, and the French are arresting all the English men they can find….

When Elizabeth and Darcy finally return to England, their relationship has changed, and they face new crises. However, they have secrets they must conceal—even from their own families.

When Mary Met the Colonel

Without the beauty and wit of the older Bennet sisters or the liveliness of the younger, Mary is the Bennet sister most often overlooked. She has resigned herself to a life of loneliness, alleviated only by music and the occasional book of military history.

Colonel Fitzwilliam finds himself envying his friends who are marrying wonderful women while he only attracts empty-headed flirts. He longs for a caring, well-informed woman who will see the man beneath the uniform.

A chance meeting in Longbourn's garden during Darcy and Elizabeth's wedding breakfast kindles an attraction between Mary and the Colonel. However, the Colonel cannot act on these feelings since he must wed an heiress. He returns to war, although Mary finds she cannot easily forget him.

Is happily ever after possible when Mary meets the Colonel?

A Very Darcy Christmas

A *Pride and Prejudice* sequel. Elizabeth and Darcy are preparing for their first Christmas at Pemberley when they are suddenly deluged by a flood of uninvited guests. Mrs. Bennet is seeking refuge from the French invasion she believes to be imminent. Lady Catherine brings two suitors for Georgiana's hand, who cause a bit of mayhem themselves. Lydia's presence causes bickering—and a couple of small fires—while Wickham has more nefarious plans in mind....The abundance of guests soon puts a strain on her marriage as Elizabeth tries to manage the comedy and chaos while ensuring a happy Christmas for all.

Meanwhile, Georgiana is finding her suitors—and the prospect of coming out—to be very unappealing. Colonel Fitzwilliam seems to be the only person who understands her fondness for riding astride and shooting pistols. Georgiana realizes she's beginning to have more than cousinly feelings for him, but does he return them? And what kind of secrets is he hiding?

Love, romance, and humor abound as everyone gathers to celebrate a Very Darcy Christmas.